DISPOSITION

by

Drew Pyke

DISPOSITION

First published in 2012 by
New Dawn Publishers Ltd
292 Rochfords Gardens
Slough, Berkshire SL2 5XW

www.newdawnpublishersltd.co.uk

newdawnpublishersltd@gmail.com

ISBN 9781-908462-08- 4

Dedication

To Despina, as this piece of work would not have been achieved without such support and muse. To my family for patience. To Ulrike for inspiration.

CHAPTER 1

The son grips tighter on his father's large right hand, trying to avoid the onslaught of strangers weaving in and around them. Laughter, chatter and muffled music engulf them with intent, forcing the boy to squeeze firmer for comfort. Gone 10 o'clock in the evening, and the city had already changed in character and demeanour. The father squeezes back to offer a warm reassurance.

The boy wears an ill-fitting duffel coat, littered with string and tissue trailing from each pocket, and jeans that have patches on top of patches on either knee. His blonde hair falls over his brow that partially covers those striking blue eyes. His smile was once famous in his village for charming the doting mothers, making the other boys befriend him immediately. That was some 8 years ago. Now, happiness was a fond memory, perhaps even considered decadent.

The father breaks away from the flood of unfamiliar faces and takes flight up several dozen steps, to a large glass building with an insignia four times the height of the boy at its entrance. The father looks at the two security guards and their shiny new guns behind the sliding doors, and then reaches down to catch the boy's attention. The father's skin looks scorched by the sun, creasing up even more as he frowns at his son, making focus on the boy's face. There are no words shared, just glances between them, given now and again when circumstances warrant it.

The boy watches his father walking away and becoming

enveloped inside the glass, watching the strange expression on the guards' faces as they eyeball his father's appearance. He stretches out his arms as the guards pat him down, sides, chest, back, inner thighs, calves and ankles. In constant conversation with each other throughout, both guards then deliver the father through a tall steel door frame, dotted with green flashing lights around its borders. The boy turns and slides his hands inside his pockets, playing with the strangles of string between thumb and forefinger and looking back out onto the pavement at the foot of the steps. The smell of pollution still has not stopped choking the back of his throat, and his eyes remain red and sensitive to the touch.

It is after several hours and a bout of rain that he sees his father appear again through the sliding doors. Walking out nonchalantly, he reaches into the inside pocket of his hooded sweater, pulls out a pouch of tobacco and begins rolling with the aid of the harsh glow behind him. The ignition of the lighter produces a sudden halo of light around his face that makes him look harsh to his son, as if something dark within has been given expression for a moment. He takes a long drag from the tip and looks upwards, releasing a breath of smoke into the chilled air which then disappears into the myriad of particles above.

The father studies his surroundings with a look of contemplation and sorrow, not looking at his son but at the large buildings that dwarf him within this big, dirty city. After several minutes, he takes the butt between thumb and index finger and flicks it several metres outwards, making several orange flashes on the wet concrete steps below. The bountiful muscles in his neck and shoulders make it hard work in craning his gaze towards his son, who is still stood in the exact same position that he was left in, playing with string in his pocket and looking longingly for expression in his father's face.

✳✳✳

The woman plunges the trowel into the earth with haste as the sun begins to beat hard on the arch of her back. The smell of lavender fills her nostrils like a perfume as it floats in the spring breeze, wafting over from a hundred feet or so away. With her right hand, she lets the seeds drop, haphazardly yet with ordered frequency, into the line of holes dug into the earth. Three rows of five metres seeded, as is the order of things on a weekly routine, until it is to lay fallow. The sweat begins to run down the inside of her arms, creating a sudden chill when the breeze touches her bronzed skin. She rips some grass with a satisfying tug and rubs the sweat from her arms and armpits. With the trowel, she covers over each hole with earth one by one, and using a tin watering can, sprinkles the lanes with a consistent quantity.

Standing upright, she looks out to her shirtless husband in the distance, driving an axe into a metre-thick oak log. The muscles in his abdomen glisten with sweat, his shoulders beginning to glow red from strain. Collecting the can and trowel from the earth, the woman walks into the house and settles the objects on the table. She empties into an undecorated glass a litre of nettle wine from a keg. She walks out through the kitchen garden, allowing the mud and grass to taint the soles of her feet, and taking sips from the cool red liquid.

"How tall are you making it?" the woman enquires whilst passing the tumbler to her husband.

The husband drops the axe by the stump and picks up his shirt, using it to wipe the sweat from his chest. He drinks the wine hungrily, letting it drizzle from either side of his con torted lips.

"Five and a half feet," he responds, pointing to his shoulders to gesture how tall it would be. He places several planks of wood into a square to illustrate the area, with a doorway at its front no wider than six inches.

"The waste enters the top," the man says as he makes a diving motion with his right arm into an imaginary box. "In two to three months, this'll make the area at the bottom hot through decomposition, which will heat the underlying water pipes. This doorway here means you get the most nitrogen rich manure for the plants."

The husband looks on at his wife's work in the kitchen garden in the near distance, and last year's flourishing sunflowers, standing tall and healthy not far from the seed beds.

"Give it a year, and we'll have this place growing from the roof top," the husband says excitedly.

CHAPTER 2

The father drops onto the wooden chair slowly, allowing his weight to settle onto the four creaking legs beneath it. The flickering light from the candle at the centre of the table illustrates to the boy the hollows and contours of his father's weathered face. The son sits with his back against the wall on the mattress at the other side of the room, and begins weaving the string from his pockets between each finger, until a web is formed that binds his hands into a prayer-like clasp. The silence is not awkward, but a blessing, in contrast with the chaos on the streets outside. The father places his pouch of tobacco onto the table and begins forming a cigarette, with his head bowed in concentration.

The poverty of the room is expressed in its negligence. Food tins, potatoes, bottles of beer and sacks of unlabelled white powder lie scattered across the floor in one corner of the room, with the toilet and sink situated at the other end ornamented with used bandages and plasters. The son watches the father drink his cigarettes gracefully for an hour in the half-light, looking at how he stares longingly at the potatoes with some intense expression of meditation and focus. No words are exchanged between them, the silence only broken by the subtle inhalations on the unfiltered rollups and the incessant muffled sounds of conversation and traffic down on the city streets below. The son always feels safe and warm within this small room with his father, but also feels nervous when intermittently checking the clock, held up by a nail on the opposing wall. As always, as the hands near 1.10am, he feels his stomach begin to churn, his head bowing in melancholy.

On time as always, the harsh buzzer reverberates around the room. The father gets to his feet and walks to the door, picks up the receiver that silences the ring and presses down on the button before walking over to the far corner of the room again, picking up two bottles of beer and three potatoes from a sack. Several seconds pass until the slow, heavy footsteps are heard walking up the corridor, with a quick pause outside the door at the turn of the handle. It is this moment for the son that acts as the realisation that the silence has broken, and that the darkness of the city outside comes within.

Like he does every day, the man wears a white collar shirt under a thick black jumper, with several symbols arrayed around his shoulders and chest. The large white letters of "Security" are emblazoned on his back and on each arm. He helps himself to the other chair in the room and sets his hat upside down, with his gloves, badge, wallet and a small black pocket book placed within its hollow in delicate fashion. The two men do not share any pleasantries or show any recognition, but go about their routine with their usual efficiencies.

The father leaves the gas stove running, underneath the disused soup tin that has since been refashioned as a saucepan. He sits back down on his chair, pulls out a knife from his inside pocket and begins tracing the curvature of each of the three potatoes with the knife's edge, made the more difficult without his fifth finger, missing except for a stub still in the process of healing. The friend takes two tins from his left pocket, and like the father, takes a knife to prise open the lid, releasing a pungent smell of fish. Each of the men work with habit and understanding of the other's task, whilst the son remains seated on the mattress with both hands still clasped together, looking up at the silent labourers.

Three plates are positioned on the table with steam pluming from the centres of each of the potatoes, tamed by the cool brine from the tuna. The candlelight dances with the competing vacuum of steam from the food, and makes the room give a sense of unease and danger. The son looks to his father for approval to eat the potato, for which he responds with a nod. The friend takes his knife and cuts the bread into three disproportionate slices, handing the son the slither, then looks to the father and focuses on the man for the first time since his arrival, eye to eye.

"I have some news," the friend says, whilst lifting the beer to his lips.

"Yes?"

"I know a guy with a contact; someone who will know *everything*. You won't miss him; he has a spider tat over his right temple; real brutal. After people began disappearing, there was a civil servant who *resigned* from the government policy unit within a couple of days," the friend says, making inverted commas with his fingers on 'resigned'. "Don't know his name or politics, where he's from, nothing. But the word is that he has come over here, like the rest of 'em. Usual story: offered role in a corporation, nice home, middle-class, mortgaged to the hilt."

"You think he will know what happened?" The father asks.

"I reckon, but let's be realistic. You've been searching for these old government ministers and civil servants for years. There is nothing to say that this guy will be any easier to find. The only difference is it looks like he should know more than the others, hence his retirement."

"If this *machine* could make people disappear overnight with no remorse, then I don't understand why they don't do the same to these people who opposed it from inside. If anything, they're more dangerous!"

The friend swigs at his beer again, downing the last third with a single gulp. "Come on. They don't harm their own. It needs detachment, a distance. It's like death, it's not the act of dying that scares people; it's the awkwardness of it. They couldn't just sacrifice their own, it would seem too real. That's why they are given jobs in these corporations instead. They're silenced in the most humane way possible: a bung. It's these same corporations who wanted this crisis in order to start the place from scratch again: a barren landscape fertile for green shoots." The friend begins to gnaw at the potato skin with an opened mouth. "And you wonder why you don't get answers."

The father slides his plate with its half eaten potato to one side and takes out his pouch of tobacco again with occasional swigs of his beer. The son watches the sorrow in his father's eyes, the same he sees every night when the darkness from the streets enters the safety of the room; when the friend offers a facade of hope which only the son has learned to be vacant.

✳✳✳

The woman strikes a match against the brick arch and offers the flame to the wood chips that cushion the logs from underneath. The crackling sound is immediate, and after several minutes, the fireplace is ablaze with a dancing orange glow and a searing heat that sends out the winter chill throughout the house. Her brother lays askew on the chair from the pain in his back, and cups his elbow, most likely broken at the joint.

"Sister, it was crazy. We were walking down the main street with the other students, celebrating with a beer and a smoke, and holding up these massive placards of his facade, thousands of us! Everyone was enjoying themselves. Strangers walked side by side, talking about how we'll get our support from our nation's neighbours and allies for the revolution. It was no longer about political survival, we were talking about new opportunities, human dignity, even legacy! It was like we stole our country back for the people to live how we wanted, and not from some scientific blueprint, dreamt up by power-hungry drones and the foreign nations intent on plundering our assets." The brother pauses to grimace from pain. "A group split off from the main crowd, and started climbing on tanks, and putting flowers in front of its tracks.

That was when it turned nasty. Real nasty."

The brother took a cigarette from his sisters' husband and received a light, his face contorting to a scowl as the smoke channelled down into his broken ribcage.

"It was revenge?" asked the husband.

"Totally, you could even see it in the way the soldiers positioned themselves. It was like they were on drugs or something, incensed by the sight of each one of us. They picked out the weakest individuals and went for it. They used the butt of their rifles to bring us down by our knees, and then torment us like a rabbit caught in a wire trap. When other students tried to protect the fallen, then they would get it twice as bad, and usually in the face. Before, years ago, they were one of us, normal people going about their daily business. But now, they are reduced to the regime through and through. When news came in that our neighbours and allies were turning their back on us for fear of reprisal, that's when they came out and put the boot in, hard. The government had slipped and got a black eye and lost everything, but now they've come back, and made a point of who has the real power."

"What did they do to you?" his sister asks, pointing at his bloodied white shirt.

"I saw them running out from the top of the road down towards us. Everyone started shouting and ran in zigzags in all directions. I tripped over the curb and fell onto my elbows. Someone tried to help me back onto my feet, but by the time I was standing upright, he had got a blow to his face. I felt a hot splash of blood and teeth on my right cheek. I went to tackle the solider around his waist, trying to make it difficult for him to use his hands, but another soldier hit me with the butt of his rifle on my stomach."

The brother lifts his shirt to show a kaleidoscope of purples, crimson and blue on his midriff.

"That took me down. He stood above me looking down. I could see that he was the same age as me, but something in his eyes and smirk made him look ageless. He placed his large toe-capped boots on my right elbow, and ground it down onto the gravel. I can still hear the sound of the bones creaking under the pressure, and then, a crack."

"Oh god!" said the sister.

"I thought he was going to pull his rifle on me, but the situation was obviously getting too racy, and he ran on, working his way with the others through the stragglers. I managed to run out of view, off down some street alley, and wedge myself between two large coal huts for shelter. The adrenalin was stopping me from fainting, from shock and the pain, and I could still hear everything on the street, some 50 yards away, to keep my focus. I was able to strip off my shirt and sling it over my left shoulder, and place my mess of an arm in its loop."

"How long were you there for? They must've been swarming the place," asked the husband.

"I was there for many hours, until it got dark and there was no sound of patrolling tanks. It began to rain and the temperature dropped drastically. I knew I had to try my luck and make a run for it out, of the centre of town. I don't know how I did it, but I headed in the general direction, towards the north, using the narrow streets, ducking behind bins and coal huts whenever I heard a crackle of a radio or the distant sound of an engine. That's one good thing about a curfew for a running fugitive: you don't have to worry about what is and what isn't a threat. Everything is out to get you."

"God my brother, how can they do this to you?"

"I am sure they were thinking the same thing when we brought down *them* down. That's how they can do this to me. For them, it's a fight for their survival, and when you're stripped down to them basic instincts you return to animal instincts. When I was laying in them gutters, amongst the rats and the rotten cores and nursing my broken bones, I kept thinking that this was no longer about politics. I didn't see ideology in that young man's eyes; I saw something irrational and purely raw."

"Will they come for you?" the sister asks.

"They already are. They would have found out names from the University, and gone on vengeance campaigns to make sure we get the message. This will be a statement for any other groups contemplating subversion in this country. It will be an entire generation of reprimands and paranoia for certain."

"You must run away. They will *kill* you!"

"But you are forgetting something my sister. They have already killed all of us, even you eventually. Every one of us on that day felt we managed to *live* again, but it was nothing more than a shooting star. They expect us to live like dogs, and not bite back when we're taunted with sticks in our faces? What sort of life will our children lead, in the sewers of rage and suspicion?" The brother reaches out with his broken right arm to rest his hand on his sister's stomach, and the innocent foetus sleeping softly inside.

CHAPTER 3

The son suddenly awakes to a harsh tug on his blanket by his father, quickly followed by a hand covering his mouth, filling his nostrils with a heady aroma of stale tobacco. The room is dark except for a dwindling candle on the other side of the room, enough to illuminate the father's narrow-eyed focus on the door in forced silence, with the son just making out his father's beating heart through the blanket. They both remain motionless, staring at the light below the door.

On the other side of the door, they can hear the sound of two or more men whispering, in an incoherent monotone. From their low and gravely pitch, they give the essence of being large and masculine, heightening the sense of imminent danger. The son slides both arms around his father's flexing bicep as he prepares the flick knife with intent, never removing his focus from the shadows of shifting feet against the light coming from underneath the door. Certain syllables and names can just about be just made out. "Quietly", "how far?", "later", "hammer", "the boy".

Another two or three minutes pass, and the son can feel the adrenalin washing over him, lifting him to an eagle-like alertness, despite waking from a stupor. The fear from within increases exponentially with each beat of his racing heart, his imaginations of murder and violence walking in and out of focus, like ghosts with deformed faces bearing down on him. Like his father, something innate begins to shine through him and forces him to scour his peripheral vision for something useful; something sharp; something deadly. He looks on the table, and catches glimpse of his father's beer bottle. Logic begins to form from within. If the room is stormed, how much time would there be to snatch the bottle by its neck, smash the base against the corner of the table, and to wield the weapon in defence, or attack? Two steps would probably be required to reach the bottle with his right hand, and a clean first attempt at a smash could be done in a single flick of his wrist. With that, a jab in the jugular or face would be enough to bring one of them down, but would require a bull's eye at the first attempt. If missed, the opportunity would be gone.

The whispering stops and there is no shifting of the feet from underneath the door. The knob twists 180 degrees and the door pushes into the chain lock, allowing a shard of light to flood the room through the two-centimetre gap. The son loosens his grip on his father's arm in preparation for the storm, and his designs to snatch the bottle from the table. His father begins to gently adjust his position, putting his weight on both legs to be able to leap towards the door like a coiled spring, knife in hand. The sound of the men is much more audible with the opened door.

"Locked," says the intruder with a hushed tone.

Seconds that seem to transcend into hours in an overwhelming sense of panic begin to pass. No voices, creaking, or breathing. They were listening in on the room for signs of life. What wasn't clear was if they were expecting an empty room, or was this to be a vengeance call? Either way, there was no time to speculate or ask questions.

A loud sharp, blistering noise explodes in the room as the lock and its steel plate are hurled across to the other side of the room with a flood of blinding light. Forced open, the door collides against the connecting wall as a man barges through into the room, with the momentum of his shoulder carrying him forward, and with a second intruder standing in the doorway behind him, dressed all in black and a shiny leather jacket. Both their frames are immense and their shaved heads and gold teeth are sufficient emblems of danger. All rational reasoning trampled on.

The father leaps from his feet quickly enough to launch himself on the first intruder, still stumbling from the momentum of breaking through the door. With his right hand clasping onto the back of the man's head, the father throws him to the ground with a fast shove. He lies there disorientated, and immediately tries to turn his head round to scope his aggressor, but the father moves first, bringing his right knee down hard between the man's shoulder blades, pinning him down and probably breaking ribs. The son watches with dread as the father raises his right arm in mid-air, flicks open the knife, and with a sudden stab downwards, manages to land the tip of the blade into the intruder's throat behind the jugular, with a responsive spurt of hot red blood spraying up the father's forearm.

The son can see the man trying to gulp air unsuccessfully as the blade begins to push outwards, applying pressure on the wind pipe, closing the only channel to the lungs. The father looks behind and sees the other intruder in a pristine suit and tie, looking on horrified through the doorway, calculating the chances of fleeing alive or attempting to save his colleague. Standing in the doorframe, he sizes the father up as he suffocates the man beneath him with his manipulating knife. His colleague is beyond repair. The situation is settled with each convulsion of the dying man underneath him, the blood beginning to gush out of the wound. His arms reach outwards to struggle and flail for mercy, but the father remains motionless, as if trapping an upturned beetle beneath a thumb and forefinger.

The son springs off the mattress and sprints to the table, taking advantage of the intruder's stunned silence. He picks up the beer bottle from off the table and studies it for a few seconds, before driving it down hard on the corner of the table, and again, until a shattering of glass decorates the wooden floorboards. With the bottle neck still in his right hand, he turns with grace towards the stranger and takes several steps towards him while he still remains motionless, focused on the dying man in the centre of the room and unaware of the boy before him. He looks down at the boy and peers deep into his young eyes for understanding, as if looking for some sort of empathy in an innocent soul, one which had not yet been tarnished by life and experience. The son looks upwards to catch the metaphysical plea in his face, but offers no solace or consolation; an empty, hollow expression is returned in a slow and graceful monotony.

The son raises the bottle into the air. In a swift movement, the jagged edge plunges into the man's face, and again, attacking the temple in rapid succession until an opening appears and access is granted within. The man holds his arms up pathetically to stop the onslaught, but the shock convulses him into a panting plea for mercy. The son reaches for the man's tie with his left hand and tugs hard to get a better angle with the glass. The man takes several dozen hits to the face and neck, until the adrenalin finally becomes overwhelmed by raw pain. He collapses to the floor at the son's feet, holding together the fleshy residues of flesh and cartilage. The son pauses, his back to his father. He drops the bottle next to the man's side and reaches for the door, shutting it and encapsulating the room in an eerie, silent darkness.

✳✳✳

The husband sits in the kitchen, sorting seeds on the table with only candle light for company, whilst his wife sleeps in the bedroom above, fatigued by the heavy kicks that now eerily protrude from her belly these days. Thousands of seeds are littered haphazardly in a heap at the centre, with the Husband taking each one individually for study. He presses hard on them between thumb and forefinger and rolls them, testing for buoyancy. It is nearing midnight as he hears a sudden unfriendly knocking at the door. Momentarily, he checks the clock above the stove, and again stares at the door, confused. He gets to his feet and narrows his eyes as he walks towards the door. An isolated house in the countryside, with few close neighbours, does not usually warrant visitors at such a time in the night.

He opens the door slowly and is greeted by men in state uniform, emblazoned with golden tags on their shoulders and silver pistols on their belts. The husband, never having seen uniform before, quickly relents and opens the door. Three of them walk in without words or warrant, leaving two more standing at the door looking outwards. The smell of leather and formaldehyde from their shiny creaky attire is putrid and alien, their demeanour downcast. There is no conversation between them or with the husband, just a sequence of nods and subtle hand gestures. All four sit on each side of the table in rickety chairs, creaking with the load of muscle and steel. Except for the husband, they all look down on the thousands of seeds before them with a quizzical look. One picks up a random seed and holds it up to the light for further study, offering it to the others with a subsequent shrug. Another one places it between their front teeth to test edibility, but soon lazily spits it onto the floor towards the fireplace. The startling similarity between each of them frightens the husband as something unnatural, and inhumanely sophisticated – machine-like.

The tallest officer assumes leadership and clicks his gloved fingers to get the Husband's attention. With the back of his right forearm, he rests it on one side of the table and sweeps it sideways, casting the seeds onto the floor to undo the hours of dedicated sorting. He then places a photograph in the centre and taps it three times with his index finger to draw attention to it. The candlelight from below makes the officer's eye sockets seem more dark and imposing. Not a blemish or fault shows on his face from underneath his peaked hat, just pale ivory skin and a mysterious set of crystal blue eyes, peering deep into the husband's inner self.

"If you tell me where this gentleman is right now, we shall walk away as quickly as we came in," the officer says in a succinct orated voice.

He then takes his finger off the photo and places both hands side by side, palm down on the table, in a seemingly disingenuous tenderness. A calmness that looks to conceal a danger from within unnerves the husband.

"If you don't tell me where this gentleman is right now..." The officer pauses for several seconds. "Then I shall take your little finger today."

The officer demonstrates the execution by showing three fingers of his gloved hand, concealing the fourth.

"My wife is pregnant. I am a farmer. I have had no trouble with the police. What do you want? Why are you threatening me? I don't know where this man is." The husband pleads.

"Is that a No?" the officer whispers, wiggling all of his fingers mockingly and creasing his perfect face with a wide grin.

"But what if I don't know where he is? What if he left?"

"We know his sister lives here. We know all these rats fled back to the countryside when they did their nasty work intown. So I will ask politely."

The officer begins to stroke his index finger over the husband's hand, sending a chill of fear through his very bones. With a sardonically sad face and a gentle whisper that was audible only for the husband, the officer continues.

"Do you know where this gentleman is...? *Please...?*"

"I am nothing to do with the city. I don't want to know what he got up to. I am on neither side of the conflict. I have got nothing to do with you. I have got nothing to do with him. I am myself and my wife and my son to be. You are you and your urban life. Please. I am guilty for being innocent. I don't want any part of it."

With a flick of his right hand, the order is sent. The officer snatches and squeezes the husband's hand, keeping it in place with a tight grip, whilst the second officer takes out a spoon in immediate succession, placing it under the knuckle on the finger. The third officer walks behind and muffles and gags the husband with a large dry sponge forced in the mouth. Then, a sharp, gristle like pain pushes down within seconds on the tendon with an awkward, uncomfortable grinding, the curvature of the spoon beginning to separate finger from hand. Blood begins to enter the long winding crevices of the wooden kitchen table, the excess draining down onto the floor with gentle horrific splashes. No more than five seconds and the little finger becomes severed from the husband's body. Adrenalin fuels his body to the extent that he can hear the blood flowing through his body like a deafening drum.

Kept back on his chair by the officer behind him, the husband begins to feel consciousness subside into a gentle drunken mist, slowly dissolving all semblance of reality, not even being able to comprehend the vomit coming out of his mouth, eyes rolling backwards into his self.

In the silence, the lead officer begins to bandage up the incessant surge of blood coming from the stump wound on the husband's hand with a tourniquet, using high-grade hospital equipment. As a parting gift, a note is slid into the husband's shirt breast pocket, alongside the sanitised little finger that produces a rose-like flower on the fabric of his shirt as the blood stains the white fibres.

CHAPTER 4

The father sits at the table as the son wakes from a deep stupor, the cascade of falling dust glittering as it catches the morning light. The father opens up one of the dead men's wallets and places the contents on the table with great symmetry, turning the cards face up and ironing out the receipts and bits of paper with the back of his hand. He takes out a thin black book from his back pocket and begins writing down every minute detail- names, addresses, train ticket destinations and portrait descriptions from ID badges. The son watches on with numb consideration, playing nonchalantly with the tumbleweed of string sitting in his right trouser pocket. In the far right corner of the room lies a heap covered with a black bin liner, with a foot and a hand poking out from underneath, stained by the oxygenated black blood.

The broken bottle neck and its shards of glass that the son used to bring down the second intruder sits in the middle of the floor with bits of bloody flesh still attached, creating a spider-like pattern in the cracks and crevices of the wooden floor board beneath. The son watches, mesmerised for several minutes by the kaleidoscopic colours, and begins reminiscing the previous night, at how the intruder gave up under the gurgling of blood until there was an awkward silence, broken only by the unconscious gasps from his lungs beyond his death. The string in the boy's hands again finds itself entangled into a tight bind, as if in a prayer or plea.

An hour passes. The father disposes all of the contents from the table into a disposal carrier bag, then places it neatly under the black bin liner. Walking to the other side of the room, he reaches down on his knees and parts the array of towels and jumpers lying over the side of the sink, to funnel his arm underneath the basin. The son watches on curiously at his father struggling to pull out a glistening cobalt antique gun, trailing two pieces of cello tape that had previously attached the weapon to the wall. The son widens his eyes at the shiny black metal, the long barrel and the trigger that looks surprisingly feeble considering the ability to take life.

"Whose is it? It looks really old," the son asks.

The father, not responding, sits back at the table, motioning to his son to sit on the opposing chair with a hand gesture.

"It was your uncle's. Many years ago." the father responds.

"My Uncle? What uncle? Why did he have a gun?" The son asks, alarmed.

"He disappeared one night and left this gun at the house. When I took you away, I decided to take it with us. You have to understand that we are not wanted in our own country, and that there are people after us because of what we're doing, or rather not doing. Our way of life made the important people very scared of us, because we chose not to live a certain way. They call us primitive and a hindrance to progress, but your mother and I knew nothing else. It was how we were brought up, and how your grandparents were brought up, and so on. They can't expect people to change

24

overnight. But now everything has gone to another level. Innocent people are dying and being hounded with the help of the companies in this country, because they want to dismantle society and what we had before. So now it's important that we look after ourselves and only us. This gun is the last resort. When *they* come back, they will not be wearing suits and carrying clipboards. That is why we are moving on."

The son looks at his father's eyes for specifics, but notices the urgency of the situation and decides to drop it. The father places the gun into his duffel bag on the outside pouch and begins placing items of food and clothing into the bag. He walks over to the kitchen area, takes three deodorant cans and pierces them with a pen knife at the base, perfume immediately wafting out into the room. He places them atop the two bodies and guides his son to open the door. He reaches into his trouser pocket for a lighter, flicks it on. Tossing it over to the heap, the light hits the deodorant with a gentle sizzle before the flame starts to spread over the mound.

The Father and Son charge out of the room and down the flight of stairs, jumping two steps at a time. They both hit the pavement panting, and immediately feel the harsh cold surroundings encircle them, the noise of traffic and the howling of commuters shouting for taxis and cutting down buses. The Father chooses a direction and heads forward on the pavement, holding his son's hand tight and keeping a persistent check on oncoming strangers for signs of conspiracy.

For hour after hour, the morning is beaten down with each footstep through the town, with no breaks or chances for thought. They persist through winding, unknown streets until the asphalt begins to merge into brown belt, and the merge toward suburbia becomes more and more apparent with each passing sports car. Dog walkers and school children stroll past them both, tossing sceptic glances their way. A policeman walks past the son, then looks over his shoulder moments after, making an undecipherable announcement through his walkie-talkie on his chest which returns a crackle and then a posh female voice: "...age?"

The father quickens his pace away from the policeman, despite the excruciating pain through his calves brought about by lactic acid. He walks past a large SUV and takes the opportunity, using the reflection to look back at the officer and check whether he was following. The policeman makes tentative steps in their direction, but stops short to make another muffled request to his colleague on the device. As they both continue forward, the father sees overhanging trees several hundred feet ahead and motions quicker, to get a good enough distance from themselves and the officer.

Evidently the time in which school children go to their first class of the day, a large stream of parents and students immerse them from the opposite direction. The father studies the direction of their stares, triangulating them to judge how close the police officer is. He is closing in, quickly. Behind the cover provided by the pedestrians, the father takes the chance, battling through the mothers and fathers, occasionally bumping shoulders, to reach the safety of the trees by the side of the pavement.

Zigzagging through the parents and their children, prams and pets, they reach the overhanging trees and shrubs. The father leans deliberately sideways into his son to steer him through into the safety of the vegetation, attracting shocked inquisitive glares from the passing mothers as they duck down and manoeuvre themselves on hands and knees behind the twigs and leaves. The father quickly cranes his neck round and watches the policeman, only a dozen yards away, exercising a gentle jog towards their hiding place alongside the pavement.

He pushes his son further through the shrubs and follows suit, tearing fabric and skin in the process. They enter a clearing in front of some woods and take the chance to envelop themselves in the tangle of bushes and branches. The soreness of the muscle burn and the cuts and bruises on their limbs make the struggle increasingly difficult, and they both collapse after five minutes on the clayish soil underneath them. Some fifty yards beyond them lies a cereal crop field, several months into its harvest.

The crackle of the radio can be heard ebbing and flowing as the policeman continues walking past their hiding place. Breathing heavily into their sleeved hands and keeping a keen focus on the patches of bustling pavement they can see through the blackberry bushes, they wait patiently for the moment of safety to come, and for the policeman to give up the pursuit.

Finally reassured, the father slides the rucksack from his back and takes out a small cellophane bag of plasters. He pulls his son's trousers up from his ankles and begins nursing the cuts from the brambles, applying the plasters over the deep wounds. The son grimaces as the salty sweat from his father's hands smears into the wounds in the process.

"Why are you so afraid?" the son asks, taking confidence to enquire from his father's comments that morning.

"It's not fear that is making us run. If I was afraid, then I wouldn't have taken us here in the first place." The father begins plucking blackberries from the bush and places them in a cup from his rucksack, passing out intermittent berries for himself and his son.

"So where are we going?" the son asks.

The father turns away from his son, as if letting the question dissolve itself through time.

"This looks like a good spot," the father responds, taking a quick look through the brambled twigs and listening out for electronic static.

✹✹✹

With bleary eyes, trying to make sense of the hazy images through the harsh morning light, the husband slides the note from his breast pocket and reads to himself.

"Tomorrow, your wife's thumb."

He manages to drag himself up onto the chair, heaving his hefty weight from off the floor. Opening up the note again, he repeats the syllables multiple times in his mind whilst studying the bandaged stub from his hand where his right index should be. Piece by piece, he begins to reconstruct the night before from the jagged fragments of faded memory. The congealed black blood on his hand and forearm still emits a metallic smell and the sharp pain swells ferociously up his arm, forcing him to grimace with each movement. The silence of the house acts as a juxtaposition for the howls of anguish from within and the screaming urgency for decision. He focuses on the scribble: *Tomorrow.* The words echo solemnly inside his brain, as if this was an endgame with no option to stop playing.

The husband walks to the kitchen counter and begins to peel back the dressing on the bleeding stub, grinding his teeth as the cloth brings up the flesh with each tug. As he turns places his hand under the gushing cold tap, a sharp shrill shoots up his spine followed by a series of expletives from under his breath. Several minutes later, he manages to numb the sensitive area completely and begins to pad it dry with a clean towel, before wrapping the open flesh and the knuckle with an array of dish-clothes and socks.

The searing heat from the morning sunlight acts as a welcome bath of vitamin D upon his sensitive skin, teasing the endorphins and serotonin within his brain. On a routine day, he would have made the walk to the unfertile plains, some five miles northwards, to plant the seeds he would have prepared the night before. Instead, the husband stands motionless in the front door frame staring at the rolling hills in the distance; the swooning skylarks above; the motionless sheep grazing on the river's edge at the bottom of the valley, and the light glinting off a small window in the far distance from an isolated house.

A half hour passes as he meditates on the gentle, rolling current of the glistening river, concluding the severity of the invasion the night before. How the tentacles of an alien city within your own country can trample over the serenity and stillness of the countryside and demand from it everything. It is then that he realises that there really is nowhere to hide; that to step outside is illegal; to be your own self is now criminal. As he stands there with a stub as a finger, and a threat of retribution for something he was not involved with, the injustice begins to consume him into thoughtful rage.

This desolate landscape populated by the quiet people, toiling the soil for their families and menial bartering, stands thousands of years apart from the dirty, violent aggressive city. The husband begins to philosophise his liberties and how now there was no choice. Why he cannot live in a place impervious to governmental designs. Why there is no longer freedom to tend the land close to nature, but only to give it up to the whims of profit and power. He takes out the piece of paper and reads it again, each time slower than the last. If it wasn't for the sound of his pregnant wife stirring from the creaking bed inside, he would idle the day fixating on vengeance.

He walks further out to the garden to look in on the house through the window, at his wife entering the kitchen. As he starts to massage the tobacco in his pipe from his seat on the tree stump, he contemplates his wife's every move as she begins boiling water over the stove, as if waiting for an action or move that would reveal some secret or conspiracy. For twenty minutes, he follows her delicate hands and her eyes hidden by the tangled, tumbling hair, until she walks out with two billowing cups of Tea, forcing him to quickly hide his wounded right hand in his pocket.

"So hot today! Those lilacs are going to wither by the end of the day," she comments.

A hesitant pause is shared between them until he breaks the silence in a hushed tone, still looking down at his feet.

"What did your brother really do?" he asks.

She looks at him with surprise, taking in the round muscular shoulders under his shirt and the stubble on his face, turning slightly ginger in the light.

"Just tell me. Please." he asks.

"My love, what is wrong with you? He told you himself. He was beaten up by them stupid guards because of a student march. What else is there to know?"

The husband turns to look at her eye to eye, trying to gauge her calmness for signs of deceit.

"I understand it is your brother, and I know what he got

from them government agents was near on sadistic. But, I don't think that is the entire story."

"What do you mean? What are you saying? Why are you asking these questions? Who have you been talking to?"

Many years together, and the husband realises that for once he could not tell whether or not his wife was telling the truth, or at least ignorant of it.

"Where is he now?" he asks.

"You think if I knew I would not tell you? You think I would not have gone there myself to persuade him to stop getting involved?"

"Listen to me. The state will find him eventually, wherever he is. It is impossible to go over the borders so he is obviously in hiding somewhere in the countryside and so long as he is, it makes everyone a potential auxiliary to whatever crime he has done. That includes *us* especially, since they would know he came here and that you are his sister."

The wife looks at him despondingly, as if the immediacy of the situation had not yet struck, but at the same time sharing some semblance of recognition that they were both in striking distance of the government. The fear of losing his wife because of deceit was beginning to weigh heavily on his mind, engendering a sense of frustration and paranoia. He looks deeper into her eyes, as if seeking out something worth discovering deep within.

"You are only weeks away from giving birth, remember? You think we should put ourselves under this black cloud by choice? You can just tell me what happened and then we can do something about it, whatever it is."

"I can't believe it. So many years together and now carrying your child and you think I am involved with whatever it is you think my brother has done. He told you the same time he told me, so stop questioning me. You don't like what he is standing up for? Is that it?" the wife retorts.

"This is not political. I want to make sure that we are safe and that includes your brother. I know there are a lot of problems at the moment and that the state has got each and one of us by the throat. But, what can I do? I am not master of that world; I am not part of any world beyond that river and those hills behind me."

"So you're saying you're jealous that you don't stand up for the things that he is defending? You don't like it that someone has higher principles than you?"

"I don't think putting a spade in the ground or lambing is any less significant than standing on a platform shouting ideology to thousands of people or throwing Molotov cocktails at bystanders to spread terror."

"Then I don't get it. Why are you so bothered by what he does?"

The husband turns slowly to look at the horizon and spots a lone kestrel hovering on the thermals hundreds of metres in the air, observing the ground, beatings its wings rapidly in quick and hurried succession yet composing itself with great stillness. The head oscillates side to side to find prey with calm measure, an opportunity to carry on its purpose with a gracious and pure dignity.

"Nothing," he replies, still concealing his right hand in his pocket, still bleeding from the knuckle down.

CHAPTER 5

The son wakes up to the sound of his father rustling through the rucksack. A half loaf of bread gets segmented into thick slices and the corned beef is pushed through the tin with a satisfying suction of air. The carrier bag of other sundry items by his side informs the son that everything had been taken from a nearby bin or skip while he had been asleep, which also explained the black woollen jumper tucked tightly around his midriff.

"I miss the flat," the son says.

The father passes the sandwich over and begins gnawing hungrily at his own, made from two slabs of broken crust. The taste is dry without butter, making it difficult to push it down the throat without gagging. The son takes a moment to peer through the bushes and thorns, checking for any life on the pavement on the other side but catches sight of a string of army ants traversing a series of twigs and luminous leaves, led by scouts and a trail of irresistible pheromone. He watches each individual, with their shiny black backs and devil-like pincers, picking up everything in its wake. Leaves three times the size of their body is carried on the way to their new bivouac home with a sense of militant efficiency.

The son looks on ahead at their destined path; at the lush vegetation, the edible larvae and smaller scurrying insects, each ordained for consumption by the sudden unstoppable invasion of this new alien entity. Everything looted and blundered for the good of their own society and regeneration, with no remorse for other species or those weaker ants left behind. The pit of his stomach begins to churn with the absurdity and horror of it. The systematic, cold and calculated orgy of destruction and murder fills him with dread, and a sense of pointlessness and futility.

"We go in five minutes," the father prompts, breaking the son out of his meditation.

The son looks back at him packing the rucksack, and then down again to the trail of ants, the lack of energy to push on from one place to the next coming to consume his energy.

They crawl through under the bushes and out onto the pavement to a humming silence, void of any mothers and pupils. Some hundred yards down the road, the Father stops at a graphitized phone box, enveloping himself with a rusting door barely on its hinges. The son rests his tired back against its frame, trying hard to make out words from the indecipherable conversation over the phone from within. Looking across the street, the son notices a school entrance, with a neat lawn and flowers along its periphery. Laughter and excitable shrieks surround the building from a playground behind. Easily a hundred or more childrens' shrill, joyous voices populate the noise within the red brick school, making the son feel awkward and uncomfortable.

The conversation inside the telephone box ends quickly with a loud bang as the phone meets the rest.

"Church," the father says hurriedly.

The father walks with a committed pace through the meandering streets, taking a dozen turns each way with no map or prompts, forcing the son to struggle in keeping up. A long and exhaustive half hour walk ends with the sight of a large steeple, between prim and pretty suburban houses. Immediately the son becomes captivated by the faultless and symmetrical designs of each finite detail within each property, from the doorstep to the conifer, the rose bush to the door knocker, pavement slab to hanging basket. Transfixed by the acutely geometric shapes and harnessed nature in their pockets of display, the son is almost left behind, failing to notice his Father strolling towards the large heavy doors of the church ahead until the last moment.

The father leans hard against the five-inch thick wooden door, sending a high pitched screech echoing across the empty hall within. The chamber becomes immediately washed with a kaleidoscope of luminous colours, flaring from the stained glass windows at the opposing wall. Looking up at the array of statues several metres high on the white clad walls, they both fixate on a large Saint Francis of Assisi, wearing a simple peasantry robe and holding a sheep, surrounded by a series of golden arches. Large white stereo surround speakers decorate the walls and a plasma TV takes centre stage above the pulpit. The pews, ordained with brown leather bound bibles, display the local commercial lifestyle magazine, with its glistening front cover image of some local glamour model that made it big somewhere else.

The father places a hand on his son's back, guiding him across to the centre of the front pew, and sits down alongside him with an unusually slow grace before bowing his head toward the icon of Christ high above the tall windows. Not having been to a church before, the son looks at his father for direction and guidance. Watching his large dirty hands clasping together to form a prayer, the son follows with intense concentration, propping his elbows up on the bible in front of him and then closing his eyes.

Uncomfortable in such strange surroundings, the son opens his right eye sneakily and gazes at the idol above; the thin scrawny torso strewn with cuts and dripping blood, his eyes staring up at heaven below a crown of penetrating thorns. The colours stemming from the stained glass depictions of Saint Peter and John the Baptist bathe the father with the three primary colours about his face and clasped hands. Both biblical characters look downwards as if floating above in a superior plane, warranting celestial respect and recompense. Dotted around the hall are etchings of Latin inscriptions, adding to the intrigue and mysticism of the space for the son as he follows the loops and dots with keen focus.

A half hour passes until the heavy door is heard creaking open again, and an equally heavy set of footsteps walking towards them at the front of the pews. Without looking, the son hears the stranger help himself to the pew behind them, given away by the sound of leather folding over itself as he sits down.

"You're playing a dangerous game my friend," the stranger says.

The father does not respond. Instead, the son listens to a rustling of cash notes being pulled from his pocket and then placed on the bible in front.

"It's all I got," the father says.

They both break out of prayer and turn to look at the stranger. The man looks surprisingly young for such confidence, although several cuts and grazes around his face show substantial hard experience. His greasy cropped hair catches the light from the stained glass windows, making him look peculiarly dangerous. It is then that he realises the subtle faded tattoo of a spider over his right temple, partially covered by the hairline. A week's worth of stubble, and a golden fang tooth which takes up more space in his mouth than it should, informs the father and son of his foreignness.

The stranger picks up the money.

 "OK, you follow me. I will put you in hiding for a couple of days, and then take you to this government agent guy you're after."

"I will tell you. I've been looking for years and not found anything. Only bits and pieces here and there which never lead to anything. I've run out of cash and now it also like I've ran out of time too. I can't afford to be strung along anymore. I am just warning you that this is it for us now. You are our last hope. I need a guarantee that I'm going to get answers. Good or bad."

The stranger stands over the father and looks down, bearing a grin that makes his golden fang tooth glimmer against the inbound shards of light. Smiling wider, he drops the notes of cash back onto the father's lap and turns to leave, not giving the father the opportunity to rebuke him.

"You think you're the only guy who wants answers?" the stranger says, whilst walking to the door.

"Come to the big white house on the west edge of the town. Don't write it down."

The Stranger tugs and prises open the door with a heave before turning for a last parting.

"Now you owe me!"

***

The husband sits on the porch alone, smoking wistfully at an ebony wood pipe whilst listening to the yearning crickets from the kitchen garden. The full moon beams down a grey light over the vegetables and the cabbage white butterflies, transforming them into dancing snowflakes. The cereal crops some two hundred yards away sway along with the gentle breeze, entrancing the husband into a meditative state. A severe drop in temperature calms the surrounding wildlife into hibernation, conjuring a mysterious silence that only adds to the fatigue.

In the distance, the husband catches sight of four sets of yellow headlights, coming over the nearby hill and downward onto the winding dirt track. The black beetle-like vehicles sparkle under the moonlight, becoming larger and more threatening as they traverse the terrain, bearing down on the husband at the front porch with a deafening roar of their angry engines. He watches the first vehicle come to a halt, kicking up a cloud of grit and rubble under its tyres and around the bodywork. The husband peers through the windscreen at the tall thin officer in the passenger seat, staring back at him with dazzling blue shimmering eyes. The driver's door opens, and a man twice the size of the officer beside him steps out, but noticeably without any form of identification about his body, just plain black fatigues.

The driver walks round and opens the door for the officer on the other side, who steps out with a slow grace. The husband watches him take a deep and considered breath with a corresponding puff of his chest as the other cars begin parking behind him, illuminating his frame with a yellow halo. He gives a wide wry smile to the husband before walking towards him, up the steps and onto the porch. The husband remains in his seat, puffing on his pipe.

"So, am I going to have to invite myself in or are you going to do the decent thing?" the officer asks.

The husband looks into the officer's eyes, shaded by the flap of his black officer cap.

"She's not here, so you're wasting your time. She's gone, like her brother."

"Men, by all means..." the officer says, motioning to the other officers behind him with a hand gesture to enter the front door. A dozen of them disappear into the house with their heavy boots stomping down hard on the oak wooden boards beneath them. The tall officer helps himself to the other seat on the porch opposite the husband and sits down slowly with a measured dignity, never breaking his blue eyed gaze. The emotionless stare continues for several moments, with a background noise of his officers tipping out shelves and drawers from within the house. The husband stares back, puffing at his pipe.

"OK then, sir. Where would she be? Or better yet, where is her brother?" the officer asks.

"I don't know where my brother-in-law is. And now the wife's got spooked and left earlier ontoday. You just missed her," the husband replies.

"Well, that isn't very good is it?"

The officer stands to his feet and turn to look out on the moonlit kitchen garden before him, at the Lettuce, beetroot, marrows, strawberries, potatoes, onions and a narrow strip of grape vines tracing the perimeter. Different species of mature tree intermittently dot the patch with a large cypress at the centre, providing a natural sun dial for the garden. The composition of shades, textures, shapes and sizes appeal to the officer immediately.

"How many hours a day do you spend on this?" the officer enquires, still facing away.

The husband studies him from behind. The black shiny leather jacket and the perfect hair line on his neck from below his cap makes the man seem almost mechanical, concealing all the flaws of mankind under a sleek synthetic uniform, as If dissolving all remnants of self-identity to a soulless rank-and-file phantom, with no allegiance to anything other than the job at hand.

"It's nature, it grows itself. Just a little tweaking here and there." the husband responds.

"You don't think that you could be contributing more to your country? This patch would not feed more than a single family at most. If you became more efficient and wide scale, you could feed others and help the cause of your nation."

"Efficient as in pull it all up, grow one single crop and ply it with fertilisers to make enough food for your lot to regenerate in the cities and make even more demands on us? Feeding the beast that shackles us?"

The officer disregards the rebuke and studies the large and high-yielding strawberries several feet ahead of him.

"All sounds particularly selfish. All this land and you feed yourself with fat strawberries," the officer remarks.

"Fast growing is a short lived exercise. Your five year plans are exactly that! Rock minerals, manure and compost make that soil fertile, not your state sponsored chemical programmes. We'll be living in deserts by the time you leave office."

"You know there are soldiers dying on the borders to keep you free to enjoy this lifestyle?"

"Lifestyle? This is how the country used to be, at a time when there was even graver danger of invasion. But we never got occupied because there was nothing here worth taking. It used to be slow, human-scale development on a day-to-day basis, with enough knowledge to keep the soil rich and the waters pure. When you build skyscrapers where there were once trees, factories where there were once villages and self-glorifying temples where there were once poppies, what did you expect? Greed begets greed."

The officer turns round to face the husband.

"You know something..." the officer says, taking a silver cigarette case from his inside jacket pocket, raising his voice over the constant clanging from within the house.

"You're very difficult. Very difficult..." he trails off as he places the filter tip in his mouth and lights it with his silver embossed lighter.

"We can't classify you. Put you in any box. It makes it even more difficult to arrest you. Your brother-in-law, on the other hand, can be easily defined and identifiable by his ideology and unreasonable demands. He wants something in particular which is a notion that is anathema to the government. That makes it easy for me. You on the other hand, are different. You really do want nothing at all, so I have no grounds to put you under my boot."

The officer walks closer to the husband and bears downward, until they remain only a foot apart. He raises his right arm into the air behind him and clicks his fingers. The husband hears the heavy footsteps from the large framed car driver coming up the steps to the porch, and then standing to the

44

right of the tall officer.

"But you have to remember, this is not about you, remember? I'm here because of your brother-in-law," the officer says, taking another inhalation on his cigarette, sending up a ghoulish chemical trail of smoke in front of his crystal blue eyes and to the candle-lit lantern above his head.

"So I will ask you one more time..." the officer continues.

"Where... is... he?"

The husband watches the tall officer turn his back and walk towards the fencing of the porch, looking out to get a better view of the kitchen garden again. The driver on the other hand remains resolute, standing on thick trunks for legs and holding up a bulging frame of muscle. Scars decorate his face, with a particularly fresh wound on his right cheek, surrounded by a purple and blue bruise that still looks sensitive to the touch. The husband notices the surprisingly shy expression on the driver's downward face, as though broken by many seasons of suppression and desperation.

The husband watches the driver nervously, anticipating the unexpected before delivering the hesitant words.

"I don't know."

After several seconds, the officer takes another deep breath, followed by a gentle sigh.

"Earn your food." the tall officer commands his driver.

Like Pavlov's dog, the driver takes a step forward, whilst constantly keeping his head down to avoid eye contact. The husband, not knowing what to do, places his hands in front of his face in protection whilst the driver stretches his right arm as far back as his shoulder can give. As fast as the husband's hot sharp gasp, the driver's merciless fist is let off, blasting through the husband's hands and right onto his forehead with an immediate blackout.

The sound of the husband's body, crashing backwards through the chair and onto the porch floor, is heard by the surrounding wildlife, creating a responsive whirl of noise from hooting owls and gnashing wild dogs.

CHAPTER 6

The father takes tentative steps as they both approach the white shingled drive to the stranger's house. The long walk though the rough town and suburbs to the west edge lays in stark contrast to the purity of the stranger's estate around them. A peacock with a fanned plumage struts past on the lawns and hides behind a man-sized conifer in the near distance. Three stories tall, the pristine white house sits under a cross-gable roof, with an adjacent parking bay showcasing two sleek sports cars and a 4x4 with black tinted windows. CCTV cameras oscillate at all angles from the lampposts and the walls, coupled with heat sensors lower down at ankle level.

The father approaches the door cautiously, the son standing back several feet behind. A minute passes until the sound of approaching footsteps is heard, followed by a series of clicks and turns. The door opens to an elderly white haired man wearing dungarees, and with several light tools bursting out of his marsupial pouch on his chest. The man takes a look at the son hovering outside on the steps and then up at the father in quick succession.

"Ah, we are expecting you. You are wanting to come inside?" the old man asks, in a shaky foreign accent.

The father looks over the old man's shoulder behind him and notices a gilded chandelier dangling down from the ceiling, the glass icicles twinkling bright in the inbound sunlight. A fifteen to twenty foot portrait of a Siberian tiger gnarling its sharp white teeth is hung up on the adjacent wall, with its white snow backdrop dotted with droplets of blood coming from the beast's fangs. The father reaches back for his son's hand and squeezes reassuringly tight as they both follow the old man's lead to enter the house.

"Is he here?" the father asks.

"You will wait, then I will bring," the old man commands, as he walks off and disappears through one of the several Indian Rosewood doors.

The son looks upwards at a series of paintings on the ceiling. Horses swoon and charge around in erratic directions with accentuated tonal muscles and gnashing teeth. Even the flared nostrils and saliva are detailed as the animals charge at each other with an apparent intent to bite one another's ankles. The son drives his hands into his jean pockets for the comfort of his constant tangled string and takes a step closer to his father, awaiting bad news from the white haired man.

The elderly gentleman walks back into the reception hall and then disappears just as quickly through another door at the opposite side. The stranger appears, dressed in the same leather jacket as he had worn earlier in the day in the church, although with much more grease in his tangled black hair. A strong odour of sweat wafts over to the father and son, intermingled with the pungent stench of cigar smoke emanating from the fat Cuban that takes pride of place in the side of his mouth.

"So you came, huh?" the stranger asks rhetorically, making

the cigar bounce furiously with each syllable.

"Is there not somewhere we can talk privately?" the father asks.

"Yeah, yeah," the stranger replies, as he walks to the largest door of all behind the father.

Both doors open to a considerably large red room. A couple of shiny hardwood desks sit on either side of the room with a mesmerising scarlet, orange and black Ushak carpet furnishing the floor with captivating detail. An array of taxidermy is displayed in bell-jar shaped glass cases along the perimeter of the room. Ring-tailed lemurs, pigmy's, bush-babies, a teeth baring Aye-Aye, and even an adult sized Tamarin with a white Mohawk, all peer inwards through their glass enclosures in eerily dramatic poses, as if frozen at the point of salvaging mercy in their last moments.

The stranger shuts the door behind them and walks over to sit at one of the desks. The father takes the opportunity to size the place up and notices the five tall casement windows behind the stranger, each with tight intersecting patterns of lead, but with triple glazing instead of the delicate stained glass; nevertheless, workable with a sharp and robust enough tool.

The stranger reclines back in the chair and reveals the golden fang tooth again in his mouth with a beaming smile. The son notices the distinctive bulge of a gun in the stranger's leather jacket where the inside breast pocket should be. Immediately he feels his heartbeat surge with adrenaline. The father, sensing his child's nerves, looks down with a glare to assure him of control before returning his focus on the stranger.

"You said in the church that this civil servant will be expecting me?" the father asks, still standing awkwardly at the other side of the desk.

"He will be, yes. He is very keen to *make* justice." the stranger replies, still showing the golden tooth.

"But, you will understand that he doesn't want to meet you in person. Can you imagine what would happen if he was ever caught doing this?" the stranger continues.

"Yes, but it is very important I speak to him." the father says.

"Let me ask you something; just something to satisfy my curiosity. Why do you people keep coming to me? You need something from him. He wants to give that *thing* to anyone who will use it. And yet you can't ever be in the same room as each other. So much mistrust and fear! You're afraid he's the government who will take you in and he is afraid that you are some sort of undercover agent to spy on deviant ex-officials. It's amazing how you people think peace can come about at all." the stranger says.

"When there has been so much betrayal in our country, can you blame us? Anyone can be an enemy, even you for all I know." the father replies.

"Are you saying there is loyalty to no-one, my friend?" the stranger remarks, making a point of looking at the son.

"A state can destroy only so much. Some aspects of man are

going to remain a constant, no matter how much fear and paranoia you create amongst the people. This is why I need to speak to this ex civil servant." the father says in an urgent tone.

"OK, OK. First though, you give me dates, times, names, anything. I don't want him coming back asking for more information, otherwise I'm really going to charge you," the stranger replies.

"I will give you everything, do not worry," the father insists. "I don't whether it's this government or our own, but I'm attracting quite a bit of attention around here. I have to lay low but I don't know how long that can last."

"Causing trouble already are we? I hope you didn't leave anything behind. You have to remember that I'm sacrificing my own safety by acting as the middle man here, I need to know that the people after you aren't going to adopt me as a second resort when you've already scampered." the stranger asks.

"Don't worry. Nothing was left behind. They were... deceased," the father says, as he rests his large palm on his son's back.

"Good! OK, here is a piece of paper and here is a pen. Write down everything you can possibly think of. Even the weather and what you had for breakfast. When you're done, go upstairs and take the fifth room on the left. This is your room for a few days until you get a turnaround from your guy. You're not allowed to leave the house under any circumstances whilst you're staying here. After contact has been made then I'm harbouring a fugitive. Even if the place is on fire, you go on the roof. You don't leave. You understand?" the stranger says.

The father nods sheepishly in agreement as the stranger gets to his feet and walks out of the room, leaving a single sheet of A4 paper on the desk and a silver fountain pen placed by its side. The father takes the pen and begins writing with rapid speed, as if trying to capture every memory in his head before evaporating them for good. The son looks on and tries to read those few words he understands, but can only decipher sporadic numbers here and there.

"Father, will this civil servant man help with what you are looking for?" the son asks.

The father keeps his head down to focus on his scrawling. The son watches his thick dirty hands moving frantically with the pen, and the responding flexes in his bicep and shoulder as he populates the page with bold loops, ticks and lines. The stubble on his face and the dirt collected on his fingers makes him look more animalistic than usual, as if morphing into an irrational beast of the undergrowth.

A long silent half hour passes before the father drops the silver pen onto the hardwood desk and puffs out a sigh of relief from his mouth. He folds the paper in half and then rests it on the desk with a kind of tenderness, making it perpendicular to the edge of the desk.

"Right, let's get cleaned up," the father demands.

They leave the scarlet room and climb the stairs up to the stairwell on the first level. The son strolls ahead and counts the four doors on his left before standing in front of the fifth with a sense of excitement. Looking back at his father, he prises the handle down and pushes it open. Both are immediately taken aback by the sudden waft of pollen and perfume swirling around them. The son enters the room and marvels at the purity of the white walls, at the buoyant crème carpet and a vase as tall as himself enclosing a forest of white passion flowers. From the ceiling drops a miniature chandelier with white steel snowflakes coming off its spiral pattern frame. The son runs and jumps up onto the bed, with a receptive bounce from the thick mattress. The father walks over to the net curtains, drawing them to one side to reveal a vista stretching several miles into the distance, up to the horizon where the skyscrapers of the distant city puncture the perfectly straight line. The son runs past behind him into the en-suite bathroom, throwing off his ill fitting trainers and socks to enjoy the chilled sensation of the marble floor.

"Can I have a bath?" the son asks.

"Too right," the father answers, walking over to the adjacent mirror in the bedroom. He catches sight of his appearance and the loss of weight around his torso, despite still being substantially larger than the average man. The dirt around his eyes makes his eye sockets look all the more hollow, and the torn, tatty shirt and jeans remind him of all the homeless men and women he had once coalesced with, in the years spent living in the inner city with his son.

The son tosses his clothes onto the floor before turning the bath taps on at full volume. He climbs inside with his naked body, allowing the cold ceramic to chill his bones in contrast to the warm gushing water rising up around his torso. Picking up the luminous yellow bottle of bath liquid, he squirts the contents onto his chest and stomach, watching the water swish and manipulate the stringy liquid to form tingling bubbles. Eventually, the water and bubbles envelope his body like a subliminal hug, a similar sensation to that which his mother used to offer as a baby. Between that and the heady aroma of flowers and essence, the son loses the battle to keep his eyes open as he reminisces on those clean days of youth in the country, playing with his parents and the slugs.

The father strolls around the room, picking up every item to study and admire. The harsh peace and tranquillity makes his every interaction with the space more audible, more significant. The clink of china, the friction of his feet against the carpet, the breaths from his mouth, the birds in the sky through the open window, the sound of the water moving in the ceramic bath from the bathroom. After so many years of chaos, noise and violence, the realisation of his own body and presence makes his movements all the more awkward and uncomfortable to understand. He sits down on the bed and shuts his eyes, screaming inside to shut out the silence.

The husband blinks his eyes to the small morning sun above. A gentle cool breeze graces his bruised and swollen face, made worse by an ache throbbing from the forehead. As he rolls over from his back onto all fours, the husband feels a stinging pain shooting through his rib cage and lets a collection of solidified blood and stringy saliva dribble down out of his mouth. Each limb feels three times heavier, and the muscles seem wasted after a long period of unknown exertion. In the process of standing upright, a series of clicks and cracks put the vertebrae vertical again, each with a related grunt and wince.

Entering the house again through the opened front door, he stalls his momentum at the sight of the debris throughout the kitchen, left by the officers the night before. Cupboard drawers broken off their hinges, cutlery snapped in half, jam pots broken into shards of glass, seeds strewn on the floor, cups with handles broken, loaves of bread split into halves and pouches of tobacco emptied into the tin sink. Each step through the kitchen delivers a crunch or grind as the Husband reaches the hallway.

Momentarily, the Husband looks down at the mess littering the hallway, where a broken vase decorates the wooden floorboards with geometric patterns of clay brown and lilac blue. The surging pain returns to deliver a reminder of the fragility of his frame, as he tries to lower himself onto both knees. With the side of his right hand, he sweeps the floorboards clean in front of him, and with the tips of his fingers begins tracing the perimeter of a particular unassuming board until a subtle gap appears. Through grinding teeth, he pushes his fingers down deeper, creating a wedge far enough to leverage the wood upwards. He keeps up the effort, his muscles burning with pain and a cold sweat rising on his brow, until the resistance eases and the floorboard prises up. The husband satisfyingly throws the wood to one side and begins opening up the adjacent boards, making an opening wide enough for his shoulders. After a brief moment to regain his composure, he nervously delivers himself down through the dark hole, through the floor, using his left foot to search around blindly to find the first step of the ladder.

With each step, the husband feels the black space drop in temperature, the vapour in the air becoming more dense and suffocating. The smell of stale water, and something organic going through the fermentation process, tinges his nostrils sharply and churns his stomach. As his right foot searches down for the floor with both hands clasped onto the ladder, he quickly feels the resistance of water against his shoe. Still cautious and wincing in pain, he allows his shoes to become immersed in the sloshing water, standing on the floor which seems to sink underfoot. Each step delivers an echo in the room, forcing the husband to realise the expanse of space as he walks to the centre of the underground room.

"It's me," the husband whispers under his breath.

A nervous ten second pause follows, until an equally faint voice comes back from the darkness.

"Are you OK?" the voice responds.

The husband sighs in relief and drops all caution as he tries to decipher where in the room the voice was coming from.

"They left a while ago, probably last night. The fruit they knocked over is as dry as your sponge cakes."

His wife takes tentative steps from the edge of the space, also using his emanating voice as a point of direction. As they each navigate through the darkness and cold water with outstretched hands, they both stop to the sudden warmth of each other's breath against their shivering faces.

"Did they hurt you?" the wife asks, feeling for his shoulders with her searching hands.

"They didn't kill me, did they? Although we do have a bit of cleaning up to do," he replies.

"Come on, let's get out of here."

As they turn towards the hole in the floor above them, the shards of natural light vaguely illuminate the floor, inches deep in algae ridden stale water. The husband looks sparingly at an array of discoloured artwork, lain half wasted in mildew and rot. Some faint images are able to show depictions of mysterious crowds, and portraits of men with big beards pinned to the wall harbouring some indiscrete insects. Underneath the art, the husband is able to make out a near destroyed bookcase complete with large red leather bound books, with the bottom row completely swallowed up by the creeping water. The husband looks at each article briefly with a saddened face. Both his father's and his grandfather's collection of philosophy were now lain waste in these underground recesses, to be rotten down away from the scrupulous sanctions of the paranoid government.

They both climb the stairs under the guidance of the half-light coming through the hole, up into the ghoulishly grey morning above. The wife turns to begin investigating her husband's face, the many bruises around his cheeks and forehead. With a single finger she traces each cut and crevice where the driver had delivered blows- enough to render him unconscious, although not enough to cause internal damage. The husband grimaces under each touch, looking deep into her eyes for something.

Before anything could be extracted from her expression, a sudden but gentle downpour of rain breaks their solace as it rattles against the frail window panes, with the supplementary breeze throwing the raindrops through the open front door and onto the littered floor.

"My plates! Why do they need to smash things? They aren't looking for anything! They just want to make a point. They haven't left a thing unturned, everything is destroyed!"

"They seem very eager to find your brother. Looks like a lot of effort for someone that hasn't done anything," the husband remarks.

"You put me in a mud pit for a whole night and I'm days away from giving birth, you think I'm in a mood to analyse why they want to destroy my house?"

"OK, OK. I'm sorry, you should rest. They won't come back if they think you're not here, and your brother wouldn't be that stupid to chance another visit anytime soon," the husband says whilst dusting off a chair for his wife, gesturing with his hand to sit.

Still frustrated with the lack of information, the husband retreats into the bedroom next door, kneeling down next to the bed. Keeping one eye focused on the doorway, he slides his hand under the bed frame and pulls out a bag disguised as a sack of old hunting equipment that he had hid there some months ago. Taking out a bundle of tangled nets and wooden stakes, he slides his hand down to the very bottom to pull out the cool hard handle of a pistol; the weapon that his brother-in-law had left behind before he fled the household. The husband begins examining it closely for clues. Pulling out the gun and bringing it into the glint of the sunshine, he focuses on the clean black barrel, the fingered trigger and the scratched handle. For several minutes, he studies the gun at every angle, feeling his hands begin to tremble at the violence of the tool.

A sudden creak from the kitchen forces the husband to panic and slide the gun in his belt behind his back. Stuffing the satchel with the nets and wood, he then pushes the bag back under the bed. He looks to the door and finds his wife standing there, staring at him quizzically.

"What are you doing?" she asks.

"I thought you would like a lay down. Like you said, you should look after the baby. Come lay and I will fetch something to eat, OK?" the husband says, without taking breath.

Fatigued from the lack of sleep during the night before,

hiding in the underground room, she concedes and collapses onto the bed, reclining flat on her back and releasing a sigh into the air above her. Taking the opportunity, the husband sheepishly motions out of the room with an unconvincing smile, making sure the gun is concealed under his shirt and behind his back. He walks back into the mess of a kitchen and sits in the same chair he offered his wife, taking out the gun and placing it on the table in front, applying the same attention in its detail as he did beforehand. *What does this mean?* He questions himself over and over in his mind. *What has he done? What is he doing? How much does she know?* Hours pass, with a series of repetitive questions churning listlessly through his brain, and a searing paranoia that his wife might be in league with, or at least protecting, a terrorist.

He places the gun under the sink, ready for any further visits from the officers, then begins cooking toast from the hob, using a fork to turn it. The rain persists against the window, and the breeze sends a further chill through his bones as he places the breakfast on a wooden tray and delivers it to his wife, still asleep.

"Wake up, my love," he commands.

CHAPTER 7

Alone in the room, the son sits close to the television. The pixels on the screen begin to merge as he focuses in and out on the glass with a squinting eye, as if discovering some esoteric trick that everything is made up of minute insignificant atomic dots, and that life itself is merely an infinite clash of specks. As he pulls out again, he focuses on three teenage girls wearing swimsuits advertising watches, with intermittent close ups of their wrists, and then back to their contrived jostling with a volley ball, then a Frisbee on some golden oasis. Ten seconds later, a man chops wood in a tall pine forest with his shirt off, then turns to the camera to pick up a bottle at his feet and sip from its toxic yellow elixir, topped by a satisfying smirk and wink. A cycle of split-second images flash past on the television with no meaning or narrative.

The son looks at their abnormally white teeth, toned bodies, wide vacant eyes and stylised movements, and begins comparing himself from his reflection in the mirror on the adjacent wall. His scrawny, thin arms and his unruly hair, cut by his father with some water and a flick knife, could not be any more opposite, making him feel all the more foreign. He picks up the remote control and begins zapping the television set with it rapidly, shifting from one visual sensation to the next.

The assault of punchy adjectives streams through the electronic music and canned applause, like a subliminal packet of data hidden in the sound waves to germinate inside the receivers' decision-making process. Healthy engine oil, a wholesome cereal, a stylish suit, a reliable biro, an explosive sports drink; a fresh approach, a dynamic change, a traditional sentiment. Each message informs the individual of meaningful change in their life without the need for experience.

Overwhelmed by the onslaught of images, the son collapses backwards onto the bed, peering dreamily at the ceiling and its subtle crème spiral pattern as he bathes in the Technicolor light of the television. Shutting his eyes, scenes from years ago in his childhood begin to dance within his mind, haphazard except for a theme of golden brown; of large fields of wheat swaying in the summer breeze; of honey dripping from the honeycomb held up by his shirtless father, surrounded by angry bees; of the kitchen table each morning, decorated by thousands of seeds and small Hessian bags the size of trouser pockets, bulging with selected seeds for germination for that afternoon; and of the choking dust kicked up in the heat of the day.

The son rolls his head to the side and opens his eyes again to look at the television, at the bold, invasive primary colours bursting through the glass television screen, attacking the optical nerve with a circus of provocation and desperation. He mutes the TV with the nearby remote and closes his eyes again, listening to the homely sounds of the tweeting birds and siring crickets that had tinted his childhood with a sophisticated delicacy. Again he drifts backwards; to the gentle sound of a breeze picking up the leaves from the kitchen garden; how the gulls would follow religiously the horse and plough as it turned the soil; the gentle patter of rain on the window pane before an onslaught; the sound of his father driving an axe through wood in the autumn, with its satisfying crunchy split of wood and the sound of two halves of oak dropping onto the woodchip floor.

The son gets up, walking over to the television set and turning off the power button to reveal his own lost expression reflection staring back at him. Immediately, he imagines his mother walking over to him and his father, from the house into the garden, carrying sandwiches and lemon water. How he would use the back of his wrist to wipe the sweat from his brow, the same way his father would after hours in the morning sunshine tending the land. Looking up at his strong round shoulders shining from the dripping sweat, and those muscular reflexes, would always remind him of a stallion's hind leg as it pushes forward into canter. Simply looking up at his father's approving smile would make him feel like a man, inches above his peers. The playful rustling of his hair by his father's large hands, or a shove in the back onto the buoyant bales of straw, would also make him feel above and beyond his equals. As he peers harder at the reflection, he realises that his father hasn't laughed or smiled in years, and that his symbols of approval have left him wanting.

He stands up from the bed and walks over to the large decorated mirror on the adjacent wall, taking in the stature of his self within the golden frame of baby cherubs and vine leaves. Looking at the awkwardness of his limbs, it quickly becomes apparent to him that his destiny is never to be as broad and solid as his father, that he will never emulate his father's physique in a city where there is no physical purpose. Food and objects come packaged and shelved with the efficiency of robots, and consumed as hungrily as kings, dissolving all notions of value.

He takes his shirt off and looks at the four bottom ribs penetrating the flesh from within, and the pair of scrawny arms bulging at the elbow like a root flare in a tree. The twisted deformation of his limbs and the stunted development of his muscles startle him, after such a long time ignoring his material being. He slides his fingers through his dishevelled, tatty blonde hair, parting it to reveal the bags under his eyes, coupled with the extreme hollows in the eye sockets to make him look different to what he expected of himself.

He walks back to the bed and lays his frame into a foetal position, using his father's shirt for warmth, and closes his eyes, giving over to the heavy toll of internal violence and sliding into a deep sleep.

The father walks in the room to find his son sleeping, with strands of blonde hair covering his face. He walks over slowly, taking great attention to avoid making a sound, bowing down to place a delicately placed kiss on the crown of his son's head and then wrapping the remaining duvet over his body. Sitting back in the chair placed opposite the bed, he spends the remaining hours of the day watching his son sleep, and following the gentle movement of his fragile ribcage as he breathes.

Occasionally, he peers down at a piece of paper enclosed in his right hand, then turns his gaze back to his son, feeling an uncontrollable smile etch itself upon his face in the comfort of his own privacy.

✳✳✳

The husband looks down on his wife, still scurrying around on her back on the bed, sweating and grimacing from the excruciating pain shooting through her midriff, intensifying with each pulsation. Blood spills and absorbs the white sheets like a budding flower, dripping into a puddle on the wooden floor. The metallic smell hits the husband in the back of his throat, and he watches in horror at the danger of the situation as she continues to wrestle with the severity of the torture; feeling every molecule within her material body intimately for the first time.

Through the rolling tears, the wife looks back for a split second at her shirtless husband, with an equal amount of blood painted on his chest and stomach, intermingled with sweat and douses of water where he had helped sanitise the tearing. His expression speaks of shock, but mostly of absolute bewilderment at the living child wriggling within his clasping hands, sucking at the air like a fish out of water. He looks down at the baby's closed squinting eyes, its wailing mouth baring pink gums and a contracted tongue. Seeing his wife collapsing into a heap of bones and flesh in a state of putrid fatigue, he takes the screaming baby out of the room and onto the porch, where the disintegrating sky colours them both in an orange hue. The refreshing evening breeze brushes over the heat of their skin instantly as he cups the baby in his two hands, looking down at every detail of his simple, minute body.

The baby's wail turns to a wet gurgling noise, emanating from his salivating mouth, with his small limbs juddering to exercise all fingers and toes. He makes his first attempt at opening his eyelids, showing the husband two black irises, peering outwards to connect his self with his first mortal being. The husband bows down further to respond, sending hidden metaphysical messages through his watering eyes and uncontrollable smile. The child responds with a clumsy unconscious reach towards the imposing white front teeth, the husband watching and marvelling at every movement of his minuscule ligaments.

Checking into the bedroom, the husband sees his wife sleeping in the cradle of cushions and blankets, but still hears her uncomfortable panting and the thundering heartbeat within her chest. Taking the opportunity of the solitary moment, the husband walks down the porch into the kitchen garden with the child resting his heavy dozing head on his shoulder, dribbling through the cocktail of fluids on his bare skin. A dancing troupe of luminous Orange Sulfur butterflies parade themselves close by as they pollinate the flowers of the garden with dedicated diligence. The six skeletal legs of a lone butterfly navigate and tickle the curvature of the husband's wet naked back, brushing its hind wings with an angelic delicacy. From an egg to caterpillar to chrysalis, the adult butterfly completes its penultimate phase in its habitat within the natural harmony of all other species, malevolent or benign, with no intelligent design or pattern other than to exist and coexist. The husband walks onwards through the path into the three foot orchard grass, taking the butterfly with him on one of his shoulder-blades and his child on the other.

CHAPTER 8

The son wakes to find his father's large chestnut eyes peering out at him from the chair beside the bed, hunching his mountainous torso forwards, his large arms resting against his knees. An unlit roll-up dangles sullenly from the right side of his mouth, with a second tucked behind his ear. No expression, just a man looking content and at ease with his destiny. The son instantly senses optimism in his golden face and sparkling eyes, driving him to stare back with an equally nonchalant but receptive gaze.

"Are we leaving?" the son asks.

"Yes." the father responds with calm sincerity.

"Where are we going?"

The father leans back against the chair and slides his hands to the back of his head. Staring intently to search for some semblance of understanding, the son sees his father's lips slowly curling into a subtle smile, making the cigarette drop downwards.

"Home." the father says with subtle sigh.

"What do you mean? Where?" the son asks, unnerved by the unfamiliarity of his father's smile.

"I mean, we're done here. We've finished with this place. Get it?"

The son frowns even more, not able to contemplate the logic behind his father's words.

"What happened? So what were we doing here?" the son presses.

"We've been trying to find your mother." the father says bluntly.

"Here?" the son shouts excitedly.

"Of course not here."

"Then why are we looking for her here, when you know she won't be here?" the son asks, starting to get frustrated.

"Because we won't find answers back home, no one ever talks. Here; here there is truth. Here are where the architects live, the profiteers, the financiers, the investors, the power mongers, all those with the blue prints."

"This is why you have been going to all of these buildings all this time in the city?" the son asks.

"We've obviously made a name for ourselves. We're now wanted from both sides."

"Both sides?"

"It doesn't matter anymore, we're going home. We know where your mum is."

"Where?"

The father folds out the piece of paper and skim reads.

"A state project. Architecture. In the capital."

"What does that mean?" the son asks.

"We will find out," the father responds.

The father stands up from his chair and walks away from the boy towards the balcony. Several strikes on his lighter are heard, then the sparkling noise of the first drag as the flame sucks back onto the tobacco and filter. The son watches onwards from the warmth of the thick duvet, troubled by the mystery of the situation. The father looks out onto the horizon with one hand on the cool steel of the gothic balcony frame, letting the droplets from above sprinkle over his coarse hand and upon his face as he peers upwards to follow the trajectory of the raindrops, shooting down in a blitzkrieg of cool bracing water.

The son turns to the other direction and focuses on a black dot speckled with red, walking up the nearside wall, traversing the crevices with its spindly legs. The ladybird's antennae search round for potential danger with measured pace as it journeys up towards the dead end, where the wall hits the ceiling. Yet the beetle carries on further up pointlessly. The son follows its expedition meditatively, falling in on himself with concentration.

"Dad," the son prompts, still facing the wall. "What happens when we find her?"

The father turns to face his son from the balcony, still dragging on a damp cigarette.

"What are you talking about? We will do what we did before. When everything was perfect."

Just as his father's words leave his lips, the ladybird takes flight into the air, fumbling with its delicate wings from under its protective and decorated covers, fluttering out of the window into the cold, dangerous rain outside.

✱✱✱

The young son gurgles and blows bubbles from both nostrils, sitting in his primitive wooden chair at the end of the table. The husband and wife look at each other across the table over steaming bowls of thick green broccoli soup, with an awkward tension. The returning brother sits nonchalantly behind them, in the corner by the stove, puffing a cigar through an unkempt beard. He pulls faces from under his cap at the baby, brandishing his tobacco-stained teeth to make the child laugh even more vehemently.

"He is as ugly as you, big sister," he coos from the side.

The wife begins picking up the mushy food with her index finger and placing it at the baby's lips, to collect it with his pouted mouth. The father continues sharpening his knifes with a spherical pebble stone, placing them in a row side-by-side on the kitchen table. Only the singing of crickets are heard, along with intermittent hoots from visiting owls.

"So," the husband says, still concentrating on the razor-sharp edges of his tools. "Where did you go?"

The brother-in-law stops pulling faces to lean back in the chair, letting a solitary *O* of smoke float into the air above him.

"Do you really understand what you're asking me? If I were you I wouldn't ask anything. For your safety, not mine."

"I take it you never left the country or you wouldn't be able to get back in again. Or would want to." The husband persists.

"Sis, who have you married? The junta?" the brother-in-law responds with a wry smile.

"And the cities would be swarming with agents, so you couldn't have stayed there either," the father continues.

"So you are suggesting I was living in your basement without your knowing, since you have everywhere else scouted out?"

With his back to the brother-in-law, the father stops sharpening and takes time to look down on his son, struggling with a large mouthful. The tenderness and vulnerability of his struggle makes him look even younger than his year and a half. With his oil ridden right hand, he reaches over to place one palm on top of his child's white blonde hair and gives it a rough ruffle, spinning his son into a state of laughter. Looking to his wife, stirring the food with her little finger and giving irregular hidden glances at her brother, he begins to wonder.

"Did you meet many interesting people on your travels at least?" the father asks.

"Well, I wasn't under a tree all this time, if that's what you mean."

"You just look very different. You look – what's the word? – *influenced.*"

His wife looks up abruptly at her husband, grimacing.

"He's come all this way to see his nephew and you give him the inquisition. Give him a break!" the wife barks.

As she turns to clean the food from her hands with a dishcloth the father watches his son pick up one of the nearby knives, waving it in the air like a wand and letting it drop down to the marry with the wood of the table to a numb thud. The wife snatches the weapon from the child's hand and glares with horror at the husband.

"Training him are we?" the wife shouts.

She snatches the child up from the chair and disappears from the kitchen into the bedroom, leaving the two men alone in the room and the half-light of the dwindling oil lamp. The brother-in-law walks over and assumes his sister's chair. A long hesitant pause is shared, heightening the tension between them, until the husband looks up with serious intent.

"No interesting people, huh?" the husband asks.

The husband walks to the sink unit and gets to his knees to slides a hand under the basin. Maintaining eye contact, he unfastens the gun from the underside of a pipe and walks back to the table, placing it in front of his brother-in-law.

"What's your point? Should you really be having objects like this with a kid in the household?"

"Should you be using weapons at all, *people's* man?"

"Again, I have to ask: what's your point? I've not been here more than a few hours and you suddenly start showing off your arsenal like I'm meant to be impressed."

"You left it behind before you disappeared the first time. I found it under the spare bed when I was tidying up the room, along with this little book of tricks." the husband continues.

The husband takes out a small leather bound booklet from his back pocket and fans it out onto a diagram surrounded by a series of scribbles outlining some form of explosive, surrounded by instructions.

"Oh dear, oh dear! You really think someone as professional as me would really leave crumbs without sweeping up? Take a minute to think about it. Some of us are giving ourselves over to a cause for people like you to bring up your young in peace and harmony. We are giving up our safety, our money, our family and friends. With all that sacrifice, you think we make these sorts of schoolboy errors? This isn't a joke, we're changing the world, whether you appreciate it or not."

The husband looks at him through narrow sceptical eyes, confused by the change in the rules of the game.

"You expect me to believe it is not yours? That leaves my wife. She was pregnant, carrying my child. It's impossible!"

"Like I said, when you want something badly you can give up everything to make it happen. With something as significant as social change there can be no stopping you. This is to make your son grow up with honest, tangible, meaningful peace and freedom. Ask yourself: is a mother's duty to their child restricted to just giving birth and rearing them or can they give them something more important? Fighting for better schools to nurture their potential with truth and science, dignified jobs, a society where you will be considered equal or at least made equal by the goodness of the civilized lot, where progress is unhindered by deluded, irrational beliefs so he can experience things only our generation can dream of. You seriously think that bathing and feeding your children is the most a mother can offer? What is the point of rearing your young if you are only preparing them for a world of fear and paranoia? She is not the first and certainly not the last to add some *value*. You are a luckier man than you think!"

"Bringing the war to us is not the best thing for a child. Why have children in the first place if you have other ambitions?" the husband asks.

"Listen to me. It's not that there is no love. She loves her son very much. Innate relationships cannot be forgotten or abandoned completely. But, you have to understand that there is always going to be problems in being complacent when you're fighting the world and the future for your son. It's not uncommon for women to give birth to provide confusion." the brother-in-law says.

"My son is a decoy? You leave us and years later you turn up and you tell me my son has been reduced to nothing but a ploy in some grand cover!" the father bursts out in anger, forcing the flickering light to dance between their faces.

"I told you, there is love. There will always be. That is

unstoppable."

"Except that the love is nothing but a by-product, secondary to some ideology that you dreamed up? So, tell me. If I picked up this knife and walked into the bedroom in there and I plunged it into her neck, you wouldn't weep as a brother? You would only commiserate as a comrade? You'd salute and click your heels and then go on your way again to persuade the country that you're the model citizen?"

"You just don't get it, do you? You in your hideaway house with no one about but cranky farmers and your fat strawberries. There are people dying for the cause, to let you have this lifestyle you choose as worthless as it is. The ends of true happiness justify the means of sacrificing an entire generation to make it happen, so that the next generation, the son sleeping in your house, can fulfil his destiny without interference from the whim of some dictatorship."

"So what exactly is it I'm meant to do? Leave my family and join the city to take up arms against the state? And what happens if I end up dead or wounded? Your new regime will come round and thank me for the bravery?"

"If you end up murdered and your family suffered, it would be your fault. You have put them here in wild desolation." the brother-in-law snaps back.

"No life? It is nothing *but* life here. Rabbits burrow, spiders weave, kingfishers swoon, the butterflies dance. No life? There is nothing in your world, just people converging through a funnel and out the other end as uniformed machines to continue the legacy of progress towards something that no one understands, not even the architects. Just keep on walking down some road of *revolution* without knowing its consequences. But the consequences are clear to us, here where there *is* life. As clear as day, we can see the consequences churning upwards from miles away and the rumbling trucks we see on the motorways far in the distance, packing the life you so despise into handy packets for consumption and hedonism so that there is nothing left of *our* land. But you lot are rotting from the inside."

"If there was no progress, then you would be stewing here for the rest of your days and the generations after you, doing the same thing day in day out. How is that happiness?"

"You put my point better than I ever could. No one day is the same, we ourselves grow through this *mundane* existence, teaching ourselves new ways to appreciate and understand the world around us. But you, it is the fixtures and fittings that surround you that change, requiring no growth for yourself to feel change and revolution. Except, when you turn round on your years and reminisce what true development you have endured, you will bow your head in shame." the husband says, feeling his tone becoming more aggressive.

"You misunderstand us. We want to stop tyranny and justice and put in its place something humane and progressive. Where people can work and earn equal wages irrespective of if they're bankers or shop floor cleaners. So that the poor are fed and watered and the disabled given equal dignity. Today, they are forgotten because they are not productive and degenerate. What have you got against that? What makes you think we are the bad guys?"

"But you will forget them only slightly less than the government do. A country is in a permanent competition with itself to produce even bigger populations, making everyone a cog in the system to churn out greater and cheaper goods to dominate the world markets. You don't deviate on this; you just argue about how the profits are distributed, you don't say anything about dignity or destiny. Do you not understand how myopic this is? Do you honestly think there is only one alternative?" the husband hits back in a hushed monotone.

"You keep your sentiments hidden well!"

"I may not understand how things work entirely here or how deep the national debt or even tax thresholds, but that isn't the point. You're dead from the inside and everyone around you in those dirty cities. That's where this rage comes from, and the reason why I don't want any part of it in my house or to have it influencing my wife and family. There is silence in this house, the true gift for a child in this world, so they can hear the *life* that surrounds them. Every time you come, you bring with you your noise."

The husband places his hand on the table, showing the stub of his index finger where the officers had lobbed it off several months previously.

"Please take your noise with you and leave, and never come

back." the husband pleads.

The brother-in-law scratches his beard with his fingers like a rake and takes in a deep breath, his ribcage expanding as far as it will go. Still keeping eye contact, he gives the husband a subtle smirk and sits there, staring intently. A tense pause falls down on both of them before he rises from the chair. As he walks slowly towards the open front door, with his rucksack slung over one shoulder, he delivers a glob of spit on the floor. Without looking round, he disappears into the night sky and through the pathway of the kitchen garden. The husband watches the erratic fireflies dancing around his ankles as if guiding his every step out of the country and into the darkness.

The husband sits motionless for several minutes before picking up a nearby Hessian sack from behind and drops it clumsily onto the table allowing its contents to spill onto the table top with a satisfying waterfall of sound. He begins filtering through each seed with his usual precision and sorts them accordingly into miniature domes at either end of the table. In the background, he hears the loud splashes of water from the tin bath in the adjacent room, and his child's subsequent squeals of true happiness.

CHAPTER 9

The son awakes again with blurry eyes, gradually managing to focus on the window pane at the far side of the room, shimmering as the light sparkles on the dormant raindrops on the glass. His father, sitting upright at his side, stuffs sundry objects with no particular order at the base of the rucksack, making it bulge from all sides. His hair, wet from the shower, occasionally sends droplets down onto his uncharacteristically clean shaven face. An exotic, expensive aroma wafts from his shirtless body, making him seem somewhat altered after so many years of habit and convention. With an air of excitement and promise, the son jumps out of bed and gathers his belongings from the corner of the room, helping his father stuff the bag in a hurried state of anticipation and thrill. The father looks back in acknowledgment.

They both walk down the stairs in their washed and pressed clothes to meet the stranger as he stands at the bottom of the steps, baring his golden teeth proudly.

"You got what you wanted and you leave us just like that, huh?" the stranger says, widening his arms to anticipate an embrace. "But be careful. You have no idea what the country has become. I understand it has got worse, if that was ever possible."

The father briefly hugs him, awkward at the sentiment before showing his appreciation.

"You're a man of your word. I won't do us the indignity of uncomfortable pleasantries. But because you have given us what you said..." the Father trails off, places a bunch of currency into the stranger's back pocket.

He momentarily steps back and looks down at the father's son, giving him a long critical glare as if analyzing his every attribute.

"Here," the stranger states abruptly, shoving the notes into the son's pockets, packed with balls of entangled string.

"Who am I to take a man's inheritance?" he says, as he gives a universally understood ruffle to his hair.

Both father and son depart the house they had been hiding in, and step onto the white crunching gravel underfoot. The crisp morning air hits them immediately, sending a chill down their spines after so many days of being incarcerated from the real and cold world outside. The son looks up at his father and the ghost of a breath emanating from his mouth.

"Where are we going first?" the son asks, taking advantage of this new vigour and openness from his father.

The father looks down at his son and slides a cigarette out from behind his ear.

"Taking an interest now are we?" the father responds, with the subtlest of smiles. "OK then. We're getting a taxi to the airport."

"Taxi? We're going on a plane?!" the son persists.

The father ignites his cigarette and puffs a thick grey plume of smoke above his head, pressing forward down the long canal of white rock. The very thought of being above the clouds and looking down begins to reverberate romantically in the son's imagination, after all the years of being underneath looking up with no sense of order or attachment.

They press on and out of the stranger's estate, through the automatic gates, onto the wild foggy pasture beyond. The urban housing and offices follow their stride at a safe distance, half a mile off to their left. In the silent walk across the outskirts of the city, the son begins analysing the thousands of spider webs that surround them on the ground, accentuated by the gentle vapour of the morning dew. The tallest of the shrubs on either side shimmer with the morning light, the immersing silk threads enveloping every opportunity on the plant for their design and deadly purpose. He watches the breeze tease the elasticity of the webs to and fro, and the eight eyed, venom fanged arachnids at their epicentres, just sitting patiently for the faintest of tugs to the hundreds of tentacles underneath their legs.

As they push on deeper into the boggy grasslands the density of spiders increments further, with webs weaved in more elaborate patterns and on greater scales. Orb webs with threads that spiral inward towards the prey begin to decorate the lower shrubs, whilst three-dimensional, seemingly unordered tangled webs begin to smother the higher reaches, with smaller spiders scurrying in the corners ready to pounce. Sheet webs catch the vapour like a layer of white steel at the very top of the trees in a complex, providing a roof of no escape for any lost and wandering insect. On closer inspection the son catches sight of miniature black holes of funnel webs, their hair-like structures providing a tempting elusive lure of intrigue towards where the awaiting spiders reside, fangs aloft.

The son looks up at his father and his altered state. No longer enjoying the cigarette, a new intensity consumes his expression, dissolving what excitement the son had burning inside. The mist separating them and the approaching hum of the road ahead begins to inspire a nervous atmosphere, the father dropping his half smoked cigarette to the ground for the wet grass to extinguish. The damp squeaking of their hiking boots becomes less frequent as they take slower, more tentative steps towards the road.

"What is it?" the son asks.

The father doesn't respond, keeping his jaguar-like focus on the road cutting across their path ahead, with its passing cars whooshing by at rapid speed like multicoloured bullets. As they approach it, they begin to become hindered by remnants of urban disposal. Food waste, chewed up plastic bottles, remains of indecipherable road signs, a single child's shoe, even animal carcasses have to be stepped over and weaved through as they near the road. The smell of carbon pollution begins to taint the pasture's pollen rich air. The son looks up again for reassurance, but sees the danger etched on his father's face, fuelling the fear between them.

"What is it?" the son asks.

All sense of hope and ambition from the morning beginning to disintegrate, they reach the roadside, and pick out a single car parked on the side, some fifty yards away. Focusing on the vehicle, the father notices the open boot, and that no-one can be seen in either the driver or passenger seat.

"Father, tell me, please," the son insists.

"Come here. Quickly!" the father says, as he runs off to the nearest bush, aside a lake besieged by poisonous barrels and bobbing soda cans. Ducking down, they both peer through the river reeds toward the car some twenty yards away, scanning the roadside for some sign of the driver or human interference. Minutes pass silently, watching the asphalt and the swaying cypress trees in front of the motor vehicles for some clue.

"Follow me. One step behind me exactly, so I know where you are at all times." The father commands from under his breath, his deep chestnut eyes narrowing under his frowning brow. He slides a hand down to the bottom of the rucksack and pulls out the antique gun, placing it within his sleeve so that only an inch of the barrel protrudes from the cuff.

They walk towards the car, each yard as slow as the last, with their hearts racing. The ground loses its purity to the array of throwaway consumables from the road, producing serendipitous heaps here and there, in accordance with the peculiar physics of clustering. Approaching the car, the father looks intently at the opened front passenger door and quickly realises that a single 5 millimetre hole has been punctured clean through it. Following him, the son notices a second bullet hole in the door behind, prompting a tug at his father's jacket. They reach the vehicle within touching distance and, acting as if bystanders, study the frame of the car, peering through the windows. Empty.

"We have to leave," the father says with urgency and panic. He envelops his son with his right arm and walks onwards at pace, tracing the curve of the road towards the city to avoid being singled out by potential assailants. The father massages the trigger of the gun in his sleeve with a sweating index finger and bows his head downward to conceal his features from the oncoming traffic, occasionally taking time during breaks in the traffic to scan the environment for threats, or for opportunities of evasion.

Cars swoop past them both, with some nervously slowing down to catch a glimpse of their awkward dispositions. The pavement beneath becomes hard on the soles of their feet as they walk faster, making the journey inwards back into the city just as tiresome as it had been getting out some days previously.

With a long enough gap in the traffic, the father takes a chance to look up fully and take in their surroundings. The sight of a lone man trailing behind them, wearing an ill fitting suit and a black tie, sends a shock wave through the father's nervous system. Watching his hurried steps pick up pace, the father instantly knows that they are now targets, forcing him to evaluate the options available ahead of them. He spots an oncoming avenue, leading off the side of the road and into a built up complex to the left. An industrial estate where hundreds of workers are likely to be working would serve perfectly for cover. The father pulls harder on his son's wrist to keep up the pace and their chance of safety.

"Need a ride, sir?" the chaser shouts at them in a hurried voice.

The father doesn't turn, and marches harder along the pavement.

"Sir! Would you like a ride?" the chaser says again, still closing the gap.

The father quickly looks down at his son and gives a meaningful glare to keep up.

"I noticed your car has broken down. I've got mine just round the corner. Come on. Let me give you a lift," the chaser asks, with each word getting louder in volume.

The son looks up at his father, trying to sense the likelihood of a solution, but only captures desperation. Something uncontrollable from within begins to stir, to take precedence. After the feeling of calm and serenity in the stranger's house for those few days, the complete turnaround in fortune wells up inside in a fit of hot anger and frustration. Now, faced with panic and violence yet again, the son clenches both fists into tight balls of pure rage.

"Excuse me sir. I said there…"

The son breaks his father's grip and turns to face the chaser, approaching only a few metres behind them. The father instinctively reaches round, trying to grab his son by the collar, but is not quick enough to stall him. The pursuer, caught in panic, reaches into his breast pocket as if about to pull out a weapon. Swept up in the moment, the son reacts, charging forwards and clawing upwards for his face. The chaser just manages to take out his pistol and pull the trigger, sending out a large echoing noise in the son's ear- but by the time he does, the son is already on him. Shivering with adrenalin, the son delivers his thumb into the man's left eye socket. The eyeball pops with a wet squelch, and the son follows through with the trajectory of his thumb, driving it in to the hilt.

Letting off a deafening wail, the man collapses to the floor, clenching at his face with his left hand in a feeble attempt to stem the flow of spraying blood. Vomit soon follows out of his mouth as he convulses in pain and shock. The son takes advantage of the convulsions, stamping down hard on the chaser's right hand and grinding it down between the bottom of his foot and the floor beneath, forcing the gun to drop limply from his broken fingers.

The son picks it up and takes time to position the barrel in the man's other eye socket, scratching the surface of his remaining eyeball with the barrel. The chaser lets off another pig-like squeal, gurgling under the bubbling of the vomit and blood entering the well of his mouth. In a split second, the trigger is pulled. A splatter of shockingly hot blood jets through the air and onto the son's dew-drenched face, as he looks down at the meat and bone of the chaser's newly exposed skull and brains. No noise but the unsettled juices of the man's innards, curdling and settling.

The son turns away instantly to take flight, dropping the gun upon the chaser's chest. He swivels on his heels, and peers down through his blood soaked fringe at the collapsed figure of his father, blood flowing from the entry wound in the middle of his forehead.

✻✻✻

The husband drives a wooden mallet down hard on a sequence of black nails, securing planks of timber to the lowest branch of an oak tree to construct a floor space metres above the ground. Holding a newly blossomed Hebe Blue Gem flower, the son brushes the tip of his index finger against the pollen rich-anthers, leaving a sticky yellow residue under the fingernail, causing much intrigue. Standing in the grass, he looks upwards at his father and the intensity of each blow, before walking clumsily towards the tree, holding the stem of the flower with great focus.

"Dadda!" the son cries out, straining his arm out to reach.

"Is that for me? Thank you son, look at those corollas! You've got good taste. Please don't pull up anymore though, your mother will be less forgiving," the father says, reaching down from his branch in the tree with equal strain and taking the stem delicately from the little hand.

The son watches his father break a smile on his golden creased face. and takes his cue to clap his hands excitedly, albeit awkwardly. The physical motion of applause tips his balance and sends him backwards onto his towel nappy, cushioning the blow.

Working for several hours in the afternoon heat, the father manages to construct a skeleton frame within the tree branches using treated planks from a single oak, whilst keeping an intermittent eye on his son scouring the vegetation in the kitchen garden. With wide eyes, the son travels the labyrinthine plants and shrubs, lifting up wayward slugs in the air to see the transparency of their bellies in the sunlight, tracing the arches on a chrysalis hanging from the underside of a twig using his inquisitive index finger, exercising his confidence by chasing butterflies bouncing up and down in the air over the nutritious cabbage leaves. The sudden shrieks from deep within the vegetation of the garden make the father laugh to himself, turning and watching the shaking plants sway as the child tugs away at their roots.

"Leave *some* things to grow!" the father shouts with a smile, making the son stop suddenly for a few seconds to poke his head out of the grass.

With the tree hut nearly complete, the father walks over to collect his son from the undergrowth of tall yellowing grass at the foot of the kitchen garden. The son meekly struggles, clasping onto a half dozen snails with an accompanying trail of wet silver hanging from his wrists. Sweat from both of their bodies feels cool against the gentle afternoon breeze, providing a refreshing chill.

"What is missing?" the father asks, standing in front of the tree hut.

The son responds by patting his head repeatedly on his lengthy blonde hair.

"That's right. We forgot the hat," the father says, still beaming. "We're going to the river to get some water reeds and feed the ducks. OK?"

With his empty hand, the son opens and closes his fist up and down.

"That's right, the ducks," he says, walking into the house.

The both enter the kitchen to find the wife hacking at a duck with a 10 inch cleaver, severing its head from its body in a single clean chop. An arrangement of herbs, fruits, flour and vegetable litter the table-top in a collage of colours and textures, with the apron equally decorated with stains.

"We're going to the river," the father states, startling his wife's eagle eye focus.

"Don't get too wet," she shouts out to their son, who still makes duck beak motions with his right hand and squeezes tight on a cluster of snails in the concealed left, providing an oozy sludge creeping down his forearm.

They begin the journey through several fields of various crops of wheat, barley and maize, between the several bountiful hills providing grazing lands for the wild sheep and rams roaming freely without reprieve or shackle. The son, astride on his father's shoulders, takes in the wildlife darting around their path, especially the powerful hind legs of the brown hares. An hour quickly evaporates with the adventure through woodlands, pasture and bog, and they soon begin to near their goal. A river streams southbound at a current that emits a sound from several hundred feet away, enough to kick off a shrill from the son who battles energetically to get down onto the ground.

The father takes out his sickle from his belt and begins to hack furiously at the nearby roots, tossing the reeds down in a bundle at a distance free of marsh and mud to prevent rot. Like a beaver creating a dam, the son takes a single reed one by one from his father and walks it to the bundle to dry, still harbouring snails in his left hand. A whole couple of hours are devoted to accumulating and bundling the reeds, all the while making sure to avoid the croaking frogs along the river side. Only the occasional splashes in the water from the fish which come up to the surface, and the subsequent rings rippling outwards, take the son's attention from the task at hand.

Finished. Exhausted from tree hut building and the hours spent cutting down reeds, the father collapses to the ground, lying flat on his bare back, and exhales a satisfying breath into the air with his eyes closed, his leather shoes dangling in the cold streaming water. The son walks over with his dirt-ridden cheeks and clambers over his father's chest to sit on top of his rib cage, looking down mischievously. He looks in his left hand at his collection of snails and picks out the most adventurous of them all, with its slimy underside and antennae pocking out of its shell. The son delivers it generously with his right hand down onto his father's half-open lips as an offering.

"Urgh!" the father spits it out, his convulsions sending the son tumbling off to the side.

The son, lying on his back like an upturned beetle, looks up at his father, spitting with horror onto the ground and running the back of his dirty hands against his mouth. Still disgusted, the father turns to his son and pokes his tongue out as far as it can stretch.

"Has it gone? Has it gone?" the he asks erratically.

Confused, the son looks back with an eyebrow raised. Unsure what to do, he looks to his left hand and picks another snail, choosing the juiciest of them all, and again delivers it to his father for food.

"No!" he shouts, horrified. "No more!" The father holds his hand in front of his son's, warding off any more offerings.

Exhausted, the father heaves over to collect his son- shuddering slightly as he shakes the remaining snails out of his son's hand- and nestles him in the cradle of his arm, turning in the direction of the river to watch the rolling water in the diminishing light. Another hour passes in pure solitude, with the father watching the migrating gulls flock over in the pink sky, and the son resting his sleeping head against his father's inhaling chest. The lapping of the water against the river's edge helps defeat the father's struggle to remain awake, and as he wallows, deep thoughts about his wife and brother-in-law return.

With some partially dried-out reeds strapped to his back, and his son wrapped around his torso with a pair of earth-covered hands, the father walks away from the river and towards the house in the dark, with just the moonlight and the billowing smoke from the chimney to guide him back. Through the hills and rough terrain, every muscle in his body aches from exhaustion and the weight, until the sight of lights from his kitchen windows spurs him on. Eventually, the father unwraps his son from his chest and places him on the porch floor, still stirring and yawning from fatigue. He unloads the reeds onto the floor for the morning's sun to dry before returning to his son, his eyes closed but still shifting towards the house.

"I'm sorry we're late. I can explain...!" The husband shouts through the half-open front door, pushes it all the way open and steps inside.

The sight of the disordered kitchen immediately stuns the husband. The same kaleidoscope of ingredients and utensils still clutters the table, with the severed duck's head still sitting alongside its body. The fire still smoulders in the background, informing the husband that it was only recently tended. Behind him, the son walks back in through the open doorway with a confused frown.

"Mama?" the son says with a raised pitch, rubbing his eyes to regain focus.

The father looks around the room for a few seconds, searching for clues.

"Honey!" he shouts nervously, trying to tease out a response from the rooms within. As he scours the kitchen table, he picks out a piece of paper, folded into four, with the two half-eaten strawberries positioned on the top creating a rosebud stain. He unfolds the four quarters anxiously, taking a quick glance at his son with his young drowsy eyes, and then down to read the eerie blue inked handwriting.

Welcome to the reprisal. We know what your wife and her brother are involved in. No more harbouring or it's your son.

A white-hot panic scorches the inside of his stomach, curdling and churning his intestines like a thorny fruit funnelling down into his digestive system. No sign of resistance, or blood, or violence, can be seen, throughout the kitchen or anywhere else in the house. He searches each room high and low for anything to explain what had happened, for his wife, and more importantly, for any clues about what was to happen next.

The son remains static on the kitchen floor, gnawing at a slice of bread that had folded over from the edge of the table with an insatiable but tired hunger. With a prevailing sweep of his right forearm, the father brushes every object off the table and onto the tiled floor, releasing a crescendo of noise and shocking his son into silence. His large bared back folds over as he collapses his head onto the table and sighs out miserably, his head still banging with pain. A strange sense of acceptance and fate burns brightly inside, but does nothing to stem the painful flames of sorrow and panic.

"Dadda?" the son asks pleadingly.

For the first time, the father responds with no reassuring smile, but with a cold, calculated narrowing of his eyes and an unapproachable hunch of his shoulders, beginning to scare the son with the intensity of the expression. The father walks over to the wall behind him and stands with his back against the cool cement, before slumping downwards, dragging himself down its coarse, flesh-scratching surface. The son walks over tentatively and places his tiny hand on his father's large muscular thigh, yearning to understand.

The distance between them lasts for hours, as the open fire mysteriously begins to alight itself in the incoming breeze, oxygenating the woodchips under the logs. A musty charcoal smoke fills the room with an endemic sooty residue, leaving the father feeling dirty and tainted.

Throughout the night the father rests his head against the wall, looking out through the open door onto the kitchen garden beyond, in the moonlight and the mocking glinting stars, as his son lays against him for warmth and security. In the small hours, bats begin to swoop past the doorway in an ascending flight, sending a series of threatening clicks through the air as if in warning. Their wings, thin spindling webbed arms, span up and down, catch the moonlight like an esoteric and foreign invasion, complete with a black shiny gloss and their bare white fangs ready to bite.

Thoughts and scenarios plague the father's mind throughout the grey night. Images of officers with violent faces bundling his wife into armoured vehicles; of the lengths they'd go to for answers; punches and kicks; spiked drinks and laced food; rape. Questions begin to haunt him repeatedly throughout the sullen darkness. Why now? What had prompted them to come again, and to specifically kidnap her? Was it something that her brother had done which warranted a reprisal of her family, or was it a general campaign to instil fear in the dissidents? But more potently, he devotes hours to wondering about the potential of his wife. What had she done to become tied up with the sort of people that the state was now seeking for vengeance? A gun and instructions for explosives, both hidden from her own husband for a cause he was yet to understand. New pictures begin to taint his thoughts: of his wife in combat slaughtering uniformed officers; looting government establishments; rallying comrades to the cause.

For this night, the usual warmth he placed on his son's skinny frame as he slept was vacant. It did not take long for the father to conclude that his wife was never going to return to the house, and that this country was now his enemy as well as hers. Surveillance will inevitably be set up on every move in and out of their land, any interaction or correspondence with the outside world will be scrutinised for terrorism. With the heartache of loss now beginning to transform itself into a distinctive state of practical precaution, he looks down at the fair hair of his son, still sleeping and breathing wheezily through his small nostrils.

As the dawn breaks through the open door of the kitchen, after hours of contemplation, fear begins to ebb into clear decisiveness. He lays his son's head onto a potato sack at his side, and rises to his feet. Looking over the silent destruction of his world at his feet, he walks into the corridor and down into the damp cellar below the house, retrieving the rucksack he had hidden there along with the loaded pistol. He then makes his way through each room in the house, picking up any essential items, before taking ten minutes to quickly gnaw at a half chicken and down a glass of fresh milk.

As he carries his sleeping son over his shoulder and strolls out of the house, into the dawning sun of the perfumed kitchen garden, the father looks back onto the house with a galvanised sense of purpose. By leaving everything behind, he now seeks to bring everything back, whatever the course and consequence of that task. To bring his family back together will be the motivation behind every step he takes away from his isolated household, and towards the frightening urban dangers which lie before him and his young son.

CHAPTER 10

The son struggles off the train and onto the loud, busy platform, with a rucksack half his size weighing him down to the ground. Weaving and ducking through the traffic in a panic, an onslaught of faces and large cases of luggage hurl themselves forward against his momentum. The glass temple of the airport opens itself for the flood, and the son steps out of the tide to look up at the yellow hieroglyphics of arrival times, set against a large black backboard with constantly changing numbers and announcements. Through the roof, he looks up at the clear blue sky, cloudless save for the swirls being painted across it by the planes circling overhead. The magnificence of it all begins to make his stomach churn.

He takes out the passport provided by the stranger in the safe house to his father and studies it for flaws. The textured cover, the series of alphanumeric digits on the identification page, the electronic chip hidden within the paper and the image of the president, watermarked throughout bearing a charismatic smile; all of them make the son marvel at the prestige. Such a loaded document begins to engender a sense of attachment, and a bizarre pride towards a polity of which the son was never aware, let alone a participant. As he joins the back of a queue several dozen deep, he watches others holding the decorated passports, brandishing them like certificates of achievement. The son begins to analyse those around him, while they in turn stare back at his ghoulish demeanour, caused by the lack of food, sleep, and the reassuring hand he once held for comfort and direction.

The son follows the shuffle forward in line, catching sight of returning graduates coming off their homebound flight for the summer holidays, still wearing ceremonial caps, being greeted by ecstatic parents taking photographs with wet eyes. Men dressed in bleached white shirts with ties half undone walk through the Arrivals Lounge close by, tapping furiously at devices in the palms of their hands, always looking down. A girl of similar age walks past, deliberately trailing behind her family and carrying in both hands a large baguette, bursting with tomatoes, lettuce, thick white slabs of chicken and delicious mayonnaise. They both share an isolated exchange, each allowing the other time to absorb and scrutinize. The son, still reeling from fear and uncertainty, returns his gaze toward the few remaining couples in the queue, and allows his mind to drift back to the horror he had left behind at the roadside with his father and the stranger in the suit. The image of his father's eyes rolling back under his eyelids, and the blood seeping out the corners of his mouth, sends shudders through his chest, swirling him in embittered grief and animalistic fury.

Suddenly, he feels a tapping on the right shoulder, his heightened nerves making him lurch forward with shock. He whips around to find the girl with the baguette looking back at him vacantly with wide eyes, still showing signs of mayonnaise smeared on her bottom lip as she creases her mouth into a smile, baring her braced teeth.

"I don't like lettuce," she says abruptly, thrusting the half-eaten baguette into the son's right hand. Just as quickly, she skips off to catch up with her family.

The son stands motionless, holding the baguette in both hands as he watches the girl disappear through the horde of strangers jostling for positions. His heart thumps heavy in his body, forcing a blushing of his cheeks and shy trembles of his limbs. He looks down at the sandwich and its bursting contents, not knowing whether to eat it, bin it or chase after her.

"If you're not going to move then I will," a stranger from behind him says with a grunt.

The son notices the large gap ahead of him and quickly fills it with ten quick strides. Still looking at the baguette, he looks at it thoroughly, before bringing it to his lips and letting his salivating mouth take the first bite. The taste of hot chicken, intermingled with cool lettuce and squelching mayonnaise, and followed by a gentle kick of black pepper, hits the back of his throat. The surprise of such generosity throws him for several moments, given the dark ghosts that smother him in this loud arena of strangers and paranoid eyes.

Eventually reaching the desk, baguette finally consumed, the son brandishes his fake passport and tickets to the orange-faced lady sitting behind it, with her jet black hair tied in a bun at the crown on her head.

"Just hand luggage sir?" the lady enquires.

"Yes," the son says hesitantly, holding onto the rucksack straps and watching the lady with frowning eyes as she types digits into the keyboard and alternating to the paperwork for verification.

The son tries to judge fate by the expression on her face and the concentration she places on the passport as he shakes with trepidation and self-consciousness. A minute of silence passes, broken only by occasional searching questions which only add to the stress.

"I hope you enjoy your flight." She beams, and offers back the passport with a partially torn ticket.

The son places the documents into his pocket and quickly walks through the myriad of shops beyond the check-in desks, far out of reach of the orange lady for fear of mistake. Leather bags, glossy magazines, buckets of sweets, hardback novels, inflatable beach toys, make-up potions and green bottles of alcohol dazzle the floor spaces, engendering great excitement among the gleaning shoppers, peering through the glass shop windows with pointing fingers and hyperactively chattering with their partners.

The son presses on and sits at the far end of the chrome plastic benches arranged like pews within the centre of the airport, watching the aeroplanes motion slowly along the tarmac on their small wheels some hundred yards away, through the large bronze tinted windows. The calmer atmosphere here, in contrast to the retail zones, settles him into a stupor as he looks at the man-sized board high above, listing the destinations and expected flight times. Two hours until take off.

The area soon becomes populated by the exhausted

shoppers, throwing down their bags of consumables with a sense of achievement, before turning their attention back to their electronic devices, which continue to receive a battering of taps and swipes with hungry fingers. The son watches quizzically at each of them, especially those of similar age to himself, and marvels at how foreign, how alien they are. How they position themselves, the clothes they wear; the excitable manner in which they interact with their friends, the detachment they show to their parents and siblings, and the indifference, or even spite, that they show to all others. Overwhelmed by fatigue and sorrow, the son begins rifling through the rucksack for his father's thick wool jumper and places it against the side of the chair to rest his head. The heady smell of tobacco and aftershave from the fabric fills his nostrils, drowning him in a thousand memories of the past.

As his eyelids gradually fall, the images of his father's lifeless body come back again to haunt him, as they had done for the entire journey from that fateful roadside event, and on the long train ride to the airport. Memories of the vitriolic pain, shaking his father's broad shoulders to try and bring him back, desperately wanting to see his chestnut eyes again for some semblance of verve, of life. With his eyes still closed, the son clenches his hands into fists of anger, feeling the flame of rage burning brightly within his belly, the same sensation he endured when dragging his own father's body through the undergrowth by the shoulders of his jacket, off the roadside and into the woods.

Drawing breath, the son takes in the musky scent from the

jumper, breathing back his father to life via the pores of his skin and lungs. Specific episodes reconstruct themselves in his brain; of jumping from his father's large shoulders into the shuddering cold waters of the river in his home country; of always running five steps behind his large legs when chasing the selected chicken for supper; of traipsing through the grey aggressive streets of foreign cities and waiting outside large glass buildings, only to see his father's rejected face and the ubiquitous solitary cigarette. The soreness of the trauma repeats itself over and over, leaving a hollow shell of a being in its wake, until he is abruptly shaken awake by a stranger, convulsing him into a reflexive gasp.

"Your flight is about to go," a middle aged man in a business suit states, bending over to meet his eye line. "I couldn't help but notice your ticket." he says with a smile.

The son looks down and notices a spillage of paperwork and string on the floor beneath him, fallen from his pocket during the unconscious adjustments in his sleep. Picking up the debris and stuffing it back into his pocket, he storms past the stranger to the assigned gate some thirty yards away, the mad dash made even more awkward by the swaying of the heavy rucksack on his aching back.

"Lucky!" the woman at the gate exclaims with a grin as she gives the passport a glance. "I was just about to make a call out."

The son, still reeling from his haunted sleep, snatches the passport back and runs impatiently through the echoing tunnel onto the plane's front deck. A lady in uniform greets the boy with strange acknowledgement and promptly scans his ticket.

"Fifth aisle on the right. Window seat." she commands.

The son navigates through the meandering chaos of people, placing their backpacks and handbags in the compartments above their heads and swapping seats between aisles. By the fifth aisle, the son looks across at the five occupied chairs to his right, and the two empty at the end. The shock of seeing his father's vacant chair hits his heart with a sting of sorrow and brutal realisation. He shuffles past the already seated passengers and sits down next to the window, constantly looking at the howling emptiness beside him. Taking the jumper again, he places his head against its buoyancy and peers outside the window. It is then that he lets the tears fall with great generosity, allowing all appeals for attention by attendants and fellow passengers to go unheeded for the entire flight back home, as he travels backwards again in his mind, back to the loving moments when his father would crease his golden face into a wide smile for his only son, in the country where he was born and happy.

CHAPTER 11

The taxi pulls up with a screech, throwing up a cloud of dust in its wake.

"Do you want me to stay kid?" the taxi driver asks in a thick old country accent.

"No," the son replies, handing over a handful of notes from the rucksack in between the two front seats.

"Sure? Looks pretty dead here." the driver insists, taking the money with a hairy hand.

The son steps out of the vehicle for the first time since being picked up at the airport in his home country; an arrangement again set up by the stranger from the safe house, which had been scheduled for both himself and his father. He offers his back a gratifying stretch after several hours of inadequate suspension and rough terrain.

Immediately the fresh air takes the son by surprise, infiltrating his every pore with a cool pure breeze. The simple stone building several metres in front of him, while weathered by damp and moss, and missing tuffs of straw from the roof, remains resolute in the face of many harsh winters. The son takes a moment to span the horizon around, at the sweeping hills and the harvests swaying in the light autumn wind. The migrating ducks overhead squawk in chants high above as they continue their flight toward sunnier territories.

He pushes the rusting gate awkwardly on its hinges, releasing a high pitched squeak. As he walks through the kitchen garden path, subsumed by overgrown grass and weed, momentary flashes jilt his brain with memories of his youth, spent rolling and playing in the undergrowth. The potato and citrus plants show the signs of viral insemination from invading aphids with their mottled leaves and stunted growth, some even reduced to black stalks, sticking out of the soil as a memoriam to a fallen harvest. Some fallen fruits, already falling prey to the fermentation process, release an evanescent whiff of ethanol into the air, mixed with the equally potent aroma of some stray pigeon corpse being cooked by the sun. The house itself, with its front door prised open by an assault of creeping ivy, makes the son stop for a second, forcing him to question how long it must have been since his father took him from this place, and how different his life would have been had he not left.

The door opens with surprising ease into the kitchen to show a parquet floor littered with brown crisping leaves, black dust covering the glass window panes, and a flapping jet-black crow, hurling itself up in the air to try and reach the safety of a glassless window on the far side, but failing from a broken wing. A meat cleaver, since rusted at its blade, sits beside a skeleton of a dead bird and a scattering of rodent droppings, each intoxicating the room with its fumes of rot. In the corner lies a bundle of medium sized Hessian sacks, half of them bulging at the sides with a complement of seeds spilling over the edges, each one surviving this place of death to provide an eternal hope of germination and life.

Walking through the narrow corridor towards the bedroom,

the son stands at the doorway and gazes wonderingly at the tired mattress slumped on top of an iron wrought bed frame, some resistant springs coiling upward out of the fabric to show its glinting spike. He slides his back against the wall, tucking in his knees to settle on the floor. Opening his rucksack, he takes out the paperwork which his father had got from the stranger in the safe house and begins reading it intently, repeating the names and addresses. He then slides out the instructions manual that his father had kept and begins reading page after page, as if trying to memorise each step. The cold begins to bite at the son's bare flesh, compelling him to wrap himself up in his father's jumper again to prevent the drop in temperature bringing about lethargy. For several hours, he pieces all the bits of information together, using them all to slowly formulate a plan.

The afternoon sky begins to turn pink and then dark, making the room turn moonlight grey before the son realises how late it is. As if spellbound under some sort of esoteric trick, he wistfully walks into the kitchen, to the prominent pine table in the centre of the room. Out of the three drawers along its side, the son picks the middle and searches blindly for tall wax candles. Finding one, he returns to the bedroom and uses his father's lighter from the bag to light the wick, which immediately flickers orange against the room's white walls.

Now with candlelight, the son takes a moment to play with his father's tobacco pouch, found during his forays into the bottom of the bag. The smell and texture of it between his fingers begins to intrigue his curiosity, encouraging him to putting the tobacco into the accompanying papers. Roll after roll, attempt after attempt, the cigarettes crumble and disintegrate between his thumb and fingers, causing both frustration and marvel. It is not until the small hours of the morning that a sufficiently tight roll-up is made for him to ignite and take his first drag, sending out a choking cough as quickly as the inhalation.

Exhausted from the countless smoking attempts and the rumbling of his belly, his mind drifts off again, but to the girl in the airport and the fat baguette of lettuce and chicken. The act of kindness spirals inwards on itself throughout his consciousness, re-shifting his preconceptions of what people are made out of and the innate interests that bind their relationships. The distant memory of his father's smiles in his youth, just before the disappearance of his mother, becomes even more painful against the innocent beauty of the young girl's selfless gesture. How much his father had changed in such a short space of time begins to petrify him, posing the possibility of his own destiny. For a stranger to express such naked benign charity was as alien to him as the act of violence had once been, before the predispositions of the urban city shook his very core.

With the flickering of the candlelight, he catches sight of the address again on the stranger's piece of paper and repeats it over and over in his mind, wondering where and what it shall lead to. *Prison*, he reads out softly. What does that mean exactly in this country? In a place full of reprisals and symbolic disappearances, a prison of any description could easily include torture, or even murder at the last resort. What condition he would find his mother in begins to play heavily in his mind, along with the question of whether she would have survived at all after so many years. More importantly though, he had doubts about the trust he was placing in the stranger's information from the safe house, and the ex-civil servant who actually gave out the names and addresses. Was he heading towards getting his mother back, or merely entering a net designed for himself and his father, at the mercy of the state?

Picking up the manual again, he follows the instructions on the yellowing pages, with its minute eerie stick diagrams of chemical compounds and cellular structures culminating at the last page with a drawing of a box-shaped device, complete with wiring and an ignition switch at the side. An array of numbers and non-descript scribbles surround the rectangle with arrows leading to each component. Using the map that had been written on the other side of the stranger's piece of paper, he traces a line with his finger, from his house on the far east of the page, towards the extreme western edge where a cross dashed in black biro ink is written. From a square piece of paper, the distance looks to the son to be manageable within a couple of days.

Satisfied in his ambition, he nestles his head down on the jumper again and watches the candlelight dance in the subtle breeze. Whilst barely keeping awake, he watches his father as a ghost-like apparition, sitting on the mattress with his back arched over as he ties his shoes from the bed. The comforting tassel of string in his pockets help the son lull himself to sleep, accompanied by an overwhelming sense that his plan in coming here was no longer about getting his mother back, but about wanting his father to turn to him and provide his golden smile of pride.

CHAPTER 12

The son opens his eyes slowly to the sound of scratching, down at the base of the bedroom door by his side. As his focus adjusts, he catches sight of a swarm of some ten to twelve black rats sharpening their long yellow teeth against the wood, only a metre from his bare feet. Their stench and the matted grey fur on their backs repel the son with horror, as he springs to his feet and quickly gathers up the paperwork with his two hands to salvage them from being savaged. For a moment, he watches the rodents clambering over each other to get at the premium positions; their devilish black eyeballs rotating round, their teasing long noses sensing the air for food or threat. Their slick hair leaves a greasy residue on the white walls, along with the trail of accompanying droppings. The son watches them for a second through morning eyes and philosophises over their purpose, how akin their hunger is to that of the human eyes he had seen in the cities.

Stuffing the rucksack with the paperwork as haphazardly as his father used to, the son walks out of the room, never once diverting his focus from the violent rats around his feet. The kitchen takes on another form in the morning light as the cascading dust from the ceiling falls through the rays of sunshine, like a thousand twinkling stars falling down onto the floor and tables. As he walks over to the far corner of the room, stepping over the rotting debris, he centres on the Hessian sacks stacked hurriedly on top of each other, taking the largest of them all to place in his rucksack. Still hungry and dehydrated, the son swiftly leaves the house through the kitchen garden and collects some blackberries and three long carrots from the only fertile corner of the estate before deliciously gnawing at them enthusiastically.

The dusty road ahead, cutting through the diverse patches of land and colour on either side, helps ease the son's heavy heart, now that such a pursuit had all the benefits of overwhelming his thoughts and preoccupations.

With the map in his pocket, the son starts to follow the blue line on his piece of paper from one edge to the other; from his home to the city. Various characters decorate the journey with their trailing livestock or animal powered carts, all of whom would have once been part of his childhood, back when he used to make such long journeys with his father to plant seeds across the land every second day. Some of their faces show signs of hardened resolve, whilst others tip their straw hats down to avoid attention and eye contact. A few of the farmers the son recognises from his youth, but they have changed over the years, their expressions more mysterious and paranoid than he remembered.

Through the farm estates, the son abruptly reaches immature woodland with trees only four or five feet taller than himself. Jilted by the bright colours and tricks of light through the leaves, he storms underneath the canopy through the narrow gaps between the trunks, trampling over brown crispy leaves and kicking at the skittering nuts around him. A circus of wildlife hurl themselves out of reach; squirrels scurry up the vertices of the branches, birds jump off their perches in the branches and flapping leaves, and even a lone fox leaves the edible corpse of a rabbit to sprint off some twenty yards ahead into the safety of a clearing.

Still suffering from the pangs of hunger, the son plucks down various fruit and consumes them hungrily, leaving a satisfying drool of juices down his chin and throat. The acidic sweetness bubbles on his taste buds as the nectar falls gloriously down his throat, satisfying that hole of hunger in his belly. He spends the next hour meandering through the young trees and taking in the illustrious environment, where even the cobwebs seem naturally perfect and inviting. In the shelter, the son takes provisions in the knowledge that the journey is not yet over, and that the hard work is yet to be completed.

After walking out of the woods under a persistent luscious canopy of autumn-tinged green leaves, the son soon notices the track beginning to disappear, under the weeds and unkempt grass. An area where the roaming sheep and wild goats no longer maintain the vegetation informs the son that the city is close by, the limbo and blurring of the boundaries between rural and urban ownership. Still sticking religiously to the map, he looks towards the large summit half a mile ahead which according to the biro line shall overlook the city once surmounted.

Climbing the steep slope, his calf muscles begin to burn bright red, as if the day's journey had eaten into the last few calories of energy left in his body. Upon reaching the top, and exposed to the vista, the son collapses to the ground, allowing his throbbing legs to recover. He takes the opportunity to look out over the landscape ahead, the small pockets of houses clustered into towns and villages, connected by a single straight thread of a road and culminating into a large city further on in the distance.

From such a height, the son looks back at the ocean of young trees in the woods he had just walked through, swaying in the breeze, and remembers how he and his Father had visited this very landscape when it was once barren and desolate. Even from above, it is easy to see the hopping rabbits and the tentative wild deer going in and out of the woods for shelter and food where there was once nothing.

Memories flood in of voyages from years ago on his father's shoulders; how he would jump down to watch him work with his wooden trowel, tearing at the dry soil at a depth perfect for a single solitary seed and then covering it over again. It was always the son's duty to pat the earth down once covered, making sure the birds and scurrying animals did not sense the opportunity for easy pickings. Although, as his father said on many occasions on such trips, they invariably did lay waste to their efforts, and more than three quarters of their hard work in such terrain would be rendered worthless. Nevertheless, the journeys remained constant throughout the years, despite the wind and rain. The woods beneath was a reminder of nature's silent gratitude.

Energised and impatient to embark on the latter stage of his journey, the son storms down the hill, with a gravity-propelled momentum too fast for his scrawny legs. An awaiting oak tree buffers the descent with a bruising collision, sending down precarious acorns around him. The son dusts himself off and checks the bag for damage before realising the peculiar ground beneath him. A perfectly straight channel of black asphalt stops unexpectedly next to the oak tree serving as a dead end. The son stomps his right foot and slides his trainer against the gravely texture. Following the trajectory of the road outwards, the son catches sight of the first buildings on either side of the street.

As he begins walking against the hard ground, forwards towards the houses, an increasing panic develops from within. The immediacy of the contrast between the lush landscape and the series of decrepit three-storey buildings provokes a scientific observation for signs of threat or conspiracy, taking in each structure as a unit of analysis.

The first house on the left emits a loud howling from every window, creating a conflagration of sound, indecipherable save for the sound of children squealing. The animation from within provides a stark juxtaposition with the stillness on the streets, given the welcoming sunshine and gentle warm breeze flowing through the corridor of bricks and mortar. *Where is everyone?* The son asks himself in a comforting mantra. Each front garden lies overgrown with unkempt grass; tarmac riddled with an array of potholes playing host to stubborn weeds; abandoned shopping carts lay strewn on the pavements, spilling out unlabelled tins.

Walking past a dozen properties, the son manages to catch a glimpse of a net curtain being pulled to one side. An elderly gentleman with an aggressive frown looks outwards through a dirty window pane, and then just as quickly pulls the curtain back again to conceal his identity. The shock of his reaction, and the disdain and fear in his aged eyes, churns the son's stomach. *Is this a net?* He asks himself, creating a seed of doubt that he was indeed set up by the Stranger from the safe house, and that he and his father were destined for capture.

More faces appear at the windows as he presses on through the flat empty road, and more chaotic noises reverberate through the seemingly cramped housing from behind the walls. It is not until he traverses the first mile of street that he encounters his first person, standing immobile in the middle of the road. Padded with plates around his frame and a protective head guard, the son first questions whether he was human at all, with all the vestiges of nature and flaws covered up. Even the gun cradled within his two hands glitters artificially bright in the sunshine against the black chrome. The son approaches tentatively, spanning the environment for escape routes.

"Papers!" the guard demands nonchalantly through gum.

He observes the black bullet-proof suit from head to toe with an array of silver plates screwed at the corners and hinges. A deep unhealed gash running from eyebrow to hairline and a dark bruise around both eyes only add to his inhuman demeanour. The son's heartbeat races with adrenaline, boiling up as he fumbles through the paperwork in the bag for a particular document supplied by the stranger in the safe house. After several seconds, he brandishes a pink laminated card with a series of names and digits on one side, offering it with a trembling hand.

"A senior card holder at your age?" the guard says quizzically, through a series of elaborate chomps on his yellow rubbery gum.

The son looks back without response or expression, struggling hard to contain his composure in the heat of the situation. The fear of failure and subsequent capture runs through his mind in a sequence of flashing images; of torture and deprivation in a rotten cell somewhere isolated and unknown or worse, sent packing over the border and back to the foreign dirty cities he had only just fled from. The trust placed in the ex-civil serviceman begins to become tested with potentially solemn consequences.

"You're either something special or somebody's son," the guard says, as he scans the boy up and down with a glance. "By the looks of you, I reckon the latter." He passes the card back between two fingers.

The son takes the card without word and passes the guard as calmly as possible, heart still thudding. The reason for the checkpoint quickly dawns on the son, as the disparity in architecture and order quickly changes. Instead of the red brick housing overwhelmed by deterioration and neglect, there stand magnificently tall glass buildings, framed by curved white steel and glass. Against each foyer, different three letter acronyms are displayed upon semi-precious metal plaques. A handful of men wearing crisp professional suits and expressions enter and spill out of revolving doors, carrying blueprint scrolls with a sense of urgency. Some of the suits take a second look at the approaching boy as they stream past in mid-flight, as if speculating his species.

The ubiquitous skyscrapers continue rising higher the deeper he delves into the recesses of the city. A mile on from the checkpoint, and the environment of bureaucratic concrete structures dramatically changes yet again. Walking past the last skyscraper, the space suddenly bursts alive with colour and noise as he enters what seems to be the city's public square, lined with shops, restaurants, monuments, statues and flowers. Pink orchids, blue irises, orange daisies and man-sized sunflowers deck the pavement's perimeter. A colossal statue thrusts itself from the centre of the square like a static rocket towards the heavens, even taller than the neighbouring skyscrapers, his clenched fist pressed against his stone cold heart.

The people, out of suits and out of their houses, litter the wide open space with trailing cigarette fumes, expressing passionate opinions to their friends with flamboyant hand gestures. Tables and chairs outside the restaurants embrace a conclave of diners, drinking deep glasses of red wine or gnawing at large slabs of red meat.

Overwhelmed by the sheer gratification of the shiny strangers, the son promptly walks to a nearby lamppost to lean as casually as possible, taking out the map from his back pocket. According to the blue biro scrawled on the piece of paper, the prison should be stemming off one of the square's many tentacles of streets. Counting clockwise in his head, he begins determining which of the eight roads his mother should be incarcerated in, then studies it intently without drawing attention.

The blue X on the map lies down along the road twenty yards to his left; an unassuming road of similar architecture to all the other roads, although with no shoppers funnelling in or out, a sure sign of undesirability. The son spots a café positioned at the side of the junction with a perfect vantage point, down the throat of the street where the prison should be.

As he walks over and enters the natural flow of the pedestrians, a policeman walking in the opposite direction measures him up with an official type glance from head to toe, unnerving him to the core as he strolls quickly to the haven of the trendy café.

"Just one, sir?" A man in black and white prompts from behind him, with an old thick country accent tinged with the awkward effort at something more sophisticated.

"Just one." the son says quietly.

The waiter walks ahead to a spare table within the restaurant building.

"No," the son exclaims quickly after several steps. "I will sit here." The son points to the furthest reach of the outside eating area, with a prime view down through the junction of the adjacent street where the blue X lays.

"Can I get you anything to drink?" the waiter asks.

"Coffee." the son replies quietly.

The son sits down, takes his father's tobacco pouch from the bag and begins rolling ridiculously shaped cigarettes, in the same vein as the night before in his old home. On the eighth attempt, he places the roll-up in his mouth and ignites the end with a long flame from his father's lighter, trying hard not to choke or splutter. With the ambition of fitting in with those around him and notching up his apparent age, the son begins dragging on the cigarette one after the other, before taking out the manual from his bag and finding a fresh page. He looks at the first set of expensive white residential houses, continuing down the street until an obscene red brick structure with barbed wire punches its presence. Although looking from an angle, the son begins sketching out its house-sized oak door, sitting inside a tall archway with a smaller louvered door inside that. A guard of similar attire to those at the city's checkpoint stands tall in front, clutching onto a rifle across his torso with his finger ready on the trigger.

Further on down the road, the son begins detailing with a blunt pencil a quarter-complete palace, being constructed with car-sized white boulders stacked on top of each other by machinery and surprisingly scrawny workers. Hundreds of figures swarm the boulders like a colony of termites, surmounting their conical mounds to construct and maintain its architecture toward a single cohesive unit. Other figures look on with their arms crossed, whilst others stand on man-sized square rocks and shout on disapprovingly at the labourers. Looking closer, the son manages to notice the shrivelled biology of the workers, and their uniform shaven heads.

The son sits back measuring in his head the distances between buildings, the entrances and exits, the ratio of bystanders to floor space, the number of houses from the square to the prison, taking down every minute detail in note form and diagrams within the few last pages in the pad.

"Sugar, sir?" the waiter says, returning with a large steaming cup of black coffee.

"No," the son answers, closing the book quickly.

Before picking up the coffee, the son takes a look at the other diners around him and their interactions with their food and friends, at how relaxed they seem within their environment under the guise of the shadowing statue before them in the centre of the square, and the ensuing palace built not one hundred yards away by what seem to be slaves. In the corner of his eye the son suddenly spots the same policeman he caught the attention of only moments previously, pacing the pavement around the square with his right hand on a holstered gun at his hip. As he walks nearer to the café, the son quickly turns his head away, and begins sipping at the slick oily coffee as calmly as possible to shield his appearance.

The reflection in the café's window pane in front shows the oncoming police officer approaching slowly. Strolling past each diner one by one, he shares a glance with each of them, waving at the receptive children and sharing pleasantries with the elderly who express a warm consideration. The familiarity between the strangers and the officer begins to unnerve the son, as if each of them operates within the same conspiracy designed by the stranger in the safe house who put him there. He picks up the coffee cup again to sip at the steaming froth, taking the advantage to look round at the policeman approaching. The officer looks at him with an ordinary glance whilst in motion, with a hint of a habitual smile. The son looks forward in shock and back to follow the policeman's reflection, fearing arrest. The officer continues past the café but makes a double take with a much more inquisitive glare than the first, as if sussing out the snake in his own terrain.

Shaken, the son quickly puts his head down and turns to the last page of the book, to the illustration of the explosive device with its notes scrawled around its edge. In a flurry, he begins to memorise the detailed measurements and long scientific names, as he has done again and again over the past few days.

Across the square, the son catches sight of a specialist shop, in amongst the hundreds of establishments on the other side. Checking his wallet, he drops a handful of coins on the table and storms over to the opposing side, making sure to take the alternate route to the policeman. The sweat and palpitations begin to worsen as the son gets caught up in the frenetic pace of the plan, and the potential deadly outcomes associated with the risks.

In the empty shop, the son catches the attention of an assistant stacking some shelves with a neurotic accuracy, swivelling the bottles and tubes round to offer the labels to prying customers. His wrinkled small eyes crease up to focus on the son through his thick rimmed glasses.

"Yes, how can I help you?" he asks.

"I need some items that you have stacked in the shelves behind your counter." the son asks nervously, before remembering his manners. "Please."

He follows the assistant to the till and begins to reel off his ingredients from memory, producing a small mountain of small glass jars and capsule boxes on the counter.

"Pest control is it?" the assistant asks inquisitively, whilst walking up the step ladder to the top of the medicine cabinet.

"Herbicide," the son says back with a contrived confidence.

The assistant grins to himself whilst facing the glass jars behind the counter.

"There we go then." the assistant says, climbing down with the last jar in his hand. "Special offer today, by the way," he continues, ringing up the price on his till.

The son looks quizzically at the price, expecting a sum that would leave him with a few notes' change in his hand.

"Thank you," the son says, turning towards the door.

"You should use a higher ratio of chemicals." the assistant shouts after him. "If you want to get rid of those weeds for good!"

Buying the remainder of the ingredients from an electronics shop, including an alarm clock and infrared remote, the son begins to move out of the square with haste. The success of the prison sketches and the composite ingredients for the explosive device fills his heart with hope as he begins the long return journey, back to the woods beyond the hill at the edge of the city. With a galvanised spirit he manages to stride with a quickened pace, through the commercial district full of suits and blueprints, and through the mysterious residential zone at the edge of the city, all the while drinking in the immediate environment and assessing its risks and opportunities.

With satisfaction he throws the rucksack onto the ground with a thud, and promptly collapses with exhaustion under the protective roof of autumn leaves in the woods. With the memories of his father planting seeds with his constant wooden trowel, he shuts his eyes, dreaming of his father's golden smile and wondering how proud he might be.

CHAPTER 13

After a sleepless night and an arduous walk back into the city, the son finds himself looking upward at the statue, piercing the swirling rain clouds high above. Pedestrians swirl around him, negotiating optimal routes out from under the fat rain drops into the shelter of their chosen shops and cafes. The overbearing edifice of the statue begins to sap the son's vigour, coupled with the haunting images of the pain put upon his mother by faceless torturers. It is the space left behind by his father which fuels his anguish the most, and the memory of his vacant eyes looking back at him after his own failed attempt to save them both from the assailant behind them. He takes a third pill of the day from his rucksack to help numb the pain, swallowing it down along with the descending rain.

Walking down the nearby road off the public square, past the two restaurants on either side, the son takes notice of the presidential palace at the other end of the street. The lack of food and sleep shows itself through his hooded eyelids, transforming him into a lost child in a big city with no means of protection, just pure and visceral vulnerability. As he catches himself in the reflection of a large building to his side, he has to take a second glance to see through the dirty jumper inherited from his father, and the ripened skin from being over exposed to the sunshine. Such a stark contrast from when he had left the Stranger's safe house back in the foreign country, with the big bath, the flowers and the kaleidoscopic television; where there was opportunity to capture rest and meditation in a clean and quiet environment, free of stress and destitution.

The son continues to walk down the road until he reaches the superfluously large gates to the prison on the left side, with two intercepting cameras oscillating toward his static position. The guard makes a chesty grunt before walking out from the shelter of the archway, onto the rain drenched pavement to meet the boy.

"Not in school kid?" the guard asks in a gritty voice.

"I'm here with the government scheme. An inspection by the ministry of civil obedience." the son says, as confidently as possible without sounding contrived.

"And I'm the president's heavy." The guard laughs.

The son slides out the pink card from his back pocket and displays it with the palm of his right hand.

"It's an engagement programme. A government experiment to employ the young from our district in roles of responsibility. It's all about the youth these days, eh?" the son says abruptly, trying to give an air of innocence from a troubled borough.

The guard, perplexed by the situation, studies the boy in the same vein as the previous guard at the edge of the city, forcing the son to conclude that each abided by the same code and training.

"They get crazier by the day. What next?" The guard walks back to the smaller door within the prison's gate.

"Don't steal anything, and I am watching you on the cam's every footstep. Any false move and you're straight back to where you came from. Got it?" the guard commands.

The son follows him hurriedly, out of the rain and through the door. A hard kick is felt on the back of his left thigh, leaving a reeling sting.

"Put that on your record!" the guard laughs, as he swings the door shut behind him.

After the echo of the slammed door behind him, the son looks round his immediate environment in the holding chamber: nothing but cold concrete on all four walls, floor and ceiling, save for a battered impenetrable steel door in front, with large fat rivets running along its perimeter. A metal plate shifts from right to left to reveal a bloodshot eye peering in through the slot.

"Yes?" the person from the other side of the door asks.

The son relays the story of the government agency programme and brandishes the pink card again, keeping up appearances despite the fatigue and hunger. Satisfied, albeit sceptical, the second guard opens a bolt from the other side and releases the door open to the son. Immediately, the calmness of the holding room is broken with a crescendo of bellows and clanging metal with a thick stench of sweat. The son stands motionless, overwhelmed by the violence of the situation, peering past the guard to the row stacked upon row of cells climbing high to the roof, each with gyrating limbs appealing for something through the narrow bars. The strip lights hanging from the ceiling sway in line with a vehicle sized extractor fan dangling from the rood, sucking up the hot air from below, making a deafening whirring noise under the shouts of the inmates. The putrid metallic smell of blood and the stale stench of urine tinge the son's nostrils, turning his already churning stomach almost to the point of convulsion.

The guard bears down on the son with a comedic smirk, feeding off the pheromones of fear.

"Welcome," the guard exclaims through grinning tobacco stained teeth.

A gulp the size of a baseball funnels down the son's throat and his eyes widen with shock, betraying all attempts at pretence with the figure of authority standing only two feet before him. As he stares upward to span the immensity of the hall, and the roof some two hundred feet up in the air, he catches sight of a community of pigeons fluttering amongst the steel rafters above. The remnants of the birds' faeces show on the floor and against the white walls, with a dependent swarm of insects feeding off its protein.

"So where do you want to start?" the guard asks, still maintaining his wry smile.

Knowing that his mother was placed in such conditions almost makes the son faint backwards on his heels. The damp stench and cramped circumstances inform him that the prison is easily beyond fifty years old, and likely to have once been a factory of sorts before.

"Any type in particular?" the guard grunts. "Maybe start with the lifers, and then we can go onto the prisoners of conscience?"

The son notices an elderly wiry man looking lost within his blue uniform with one arm hanging out of the cell's bars, a series of tattoos spinning around his grey forearm. His face, slumped against the wall, looks back at the son with a drugged expression, then slowly allows his gaze drop to the floor in shame.

"The political prisoners, yes." the son demands instantly.

"You're the boss." the guard barks back through the overbearing noise.

The son follows the heavy clomping boots of the guard, leading him toward a dimly lit corridor with another community of cells. Within each of the rooms there are between four to five people, with only one bunker and a single toilet in the far corner. Dog bowls are padlocked to the bars, containing a watery brown sludge with chunks of some form of protein floating above its surface. The son analyzes the inmates' faces bearing back at him, with their scars of torture and the emotional vacancy of their expressions. Some shout out expletives, exerting their revenge on a weaker being to regain some semblance of dignity and prowess, a facet that they have evidently been stripped of; others plea with clasping hands for salvation, sliding their arms through the bars and extending their open palms, trying to couch the boy inwards to hear their stories of loss and failure. *How could mum ever survive this hell?* The boy asks himself when looking into the eyes of the fearful strangers. *I wish she died rather than endure this.*

"Up here!" the guard shouts over the noise, trying to get the attention of the son. In a daze, he begins climbing the steps up to the next layer.

"These are the bastards," the guard grumbles with a pointing finger.

The feeling of seeing his mother in a cell with terrorists and uncompromising fundamentalists begins to haunt his spirit more with each passing chamber. The detainees on the second tier seem vastly different from those beneath. There was little frustration or vengeance burning in their eyes, but more of a relaxed sense of acceptance, tinged with a glimmer of hope that spurred them onward. Their clothes show signs of fatigue, their faces dirty and unnourished, but nevertheless more dignified than the common criminals and murderers beneath them. The son slides out his notepad and begins writing notes as if churning through some bureaucratic form, but in fact beginning to map out the floor plan and designs of the cells, taking in every detail available; where the beds are positioned, the width of the doors, the number of the cells for each corridor, average number of detainees per chamber, even the average amount of sludge per bowl.

The son exhausts the length of the corridor and lets out a physical sigh of relief through a puff of his cheeks.

"Are you alright kid?" the guard asks loudly.

"Are these all of the political prisoners?" the son asks

defiantly.

"Not at all, we have some on work duty at the palace. They're not back until tomorrow."

"Tomorrow? So where do they sleep?" the son asks, seeking opportunity.

"Outside, they work through the night."

"But it's raining!"

"You think the penal system is seasonal?" the guard barks back aggressively.

"I think I'm done here," the son says coyly, closing his pad of notes.

"But we haven't done the other three tiers. I thought you wanted to do an inspection."

"More of a snapshot; I'm done now, thank you for your time."

The sense of failure begins to bubble up inside, along with the equally fierce need to escape the stares and howls of the inmates, the stench and the faeces, the hopelessness and the rage. The guard dejectedly walks him back down the stairs and out to the holding room, turning the key clockwise. The son stands there motionless, trembling from the exhaustion of it all, yearning for the fresh air of the countryside and the peace and quiet of the rolling green hills beneath the swooning canopy of trees.

The guard outside unlocks the door from the other side of

the holding chamber, allowing the son to walk out onto the street still awash with the rain.

"That was quick!" the guard says abruptly, holding the fat ring of keys in his hand.

"It's just a quick report," the son answers softly and delivers himself into the bourgeoning puddle outside, in the direction of the public square.

"Don't forget to visit again!" the guard shouts after him mockingly.

The son bursts into the square with a hurried sprint, bumping into several passers-by in his momentum, trying to get as much distance between the hell of the prison and himself as possible whilst purging himself with the clean, cool deluge of rain from the heavens above. A thrall of oncoming traffic bears down on him with frowning eyebrows and second glances.

He pushes down on his ankles and speeds off to escape the roar of the square. On his fifth stride, the son gets knocked back off his feet, the blow coming from a collision with a stranger in a suit. Startled, sprawling on his back, he looks up to see the familiar moustachioed pale face of the policeman, offering a hand to help him up, with a sympathetic look in his dark eyes.

The son denies the gesture, clambering back on his feet with his elbows and just as quickly fleeing past the uniformed policeman, running as fast as he can until shaded by the safety of the green trees. Only then does he collapse to the floor, allowing the lactic acid in his thighs to throb and burn bright.

⁂

The policeman watches the boy disappearing through the flood of pedestrians towards the straight road out of the city, running through the financial quarter and the poverty stricken outskirts. Shaken, he looks down to the floor where the boy fell and notices a small Hessian sack lying on the wet pavement, picking it up to study it. As he opens the fastening string, a small sprinkle of seeds falls through his fingers and onto the floor. He looks down at them with intrigue, at the simplicity and unpretentiousness of the small oval shaped kernels, and begins questioning what the erratic boy he had seen several times over the past days would want with them.

Still bemused, the policeman pockets the sack and walks off to cover his usual route around the public square, smiling and engaging with his usual wanderers, all the time with the boy's impaling expression and lanky blonde hair haunting his thoughts. *Where was he from? Why in a hurry? What circumstances made him bolt so quickly? Where was he going?* Questions swarm his mind like an intoxicating perfume. From his skills adopted in police training, he begins to piece together the information to form clues.

The boy's textured skin and wide eyed glare showed his ancestry and nurturing beyond the city's spectre of conformity. His tattered clothing showed that he was sleeping rough and likely without a guardian. However, despite the vagrancy of his state and the fear in his face, the policeman doesn't conclude him to be a threat or potential terrorist; on the contrary, he was a lost soul in need of salvation, of the civilised kind. The policeman completes his round, chatting with the local shoppers, servicemen, shop assistants and sweepers, conjuring up a smile when it was polite and necessary.

Hours later, he takes his car from one of the many tentacles of spawning streets off the square, and begin the journey back to his suburban house in his tinted bullet-proof vehicle. He leaves the epicentre of the city with its sprawling glitter and aspiration, and drives out through the inner city housing quarters, where the cheap labour live and breed in decrepit high-rise tower blocks. The policeman puts his head down and presses down on the accelerator to phase out the distress and squalor; the gushing burst pipelines, the upturned shopping trolleys, the forgotten children hugging the bus stops for shelter, and the elderly couples looking on in routine shock, fearful of the neighbourhood they were once confident in.

The policeman drives several miles outward and pulls up at his two storey detached house, complete with the picket fence around its lime green lawn, and the miniature slide delivering a child at a time down to the floor with a gratifying bump. The three sons look up to the sound of the purring engine and run towards the car with excitable glee. Their faces full of mud and drooling candy sugar, they attack the vehicle from all angles, immediately ambushing the policeman as he climbs out of the bucket seat.

"Have you left any earth for the garden?" the father asks, beaming with a smile as he collects one of them on his back.

All four reach the house with a burst of noise and activity, each sending their shoes scuttling through the hallway and entering the large living room, where the policeman's wife is found tanning herself, partially hidden by the enveloping roof above her outstretched body. The effervescent blue light storms the carpet and wall, as if breathing a cloud of electricity into the immediate atmosphere.

"One day you'll be bacon," the policeman says on entering the room, throwing his bag onto the nearest available couch.

"You're late." the woman muffles in a vitriolic tone.

"Mummy's been under there since we got home from school," one of the sons says proudly, as if declaring an act of treason.

The father begins hunting his sons with a bear-like grunt and arched back, mimicking a mammal hunting its prey with clawing fingers. Each of them scatter themselves out through the house in heightened and excitable fear of capture, giggling and short of breath. The father moves about the ground floor quietly, elaborately tossing pillows to one side and upturning boxes in the search for his children. In the kitchen he hears a pair of feet adjusting themselves, trying to keep out of view under the table. The policeman approaches on his tiptoes and stands there stationary, bowing his head to look underneath at the two odd socks, attached to a pair of thin bruise laden legs.

"Got you!" the policeman bawls, lunging down to grab the two scrawny ankles.

The boy twists in convulsions and flips himself round on his back, kicking back a feeble defence. The policeman suddenly catches sight of his energetic face and wide-eyed surprise, and is immediately taken aback by his likeness with the boy with the seeds, panicking in the public square earlier on in the day, complete with the floppy blonde hair and the thin limbs. The hollow feeling of sympathy begins to wash over him again, and the consuming questions repeat themselves cyclically in his mind; where had the boy come from, and why was he in such a state of fear and loss?

The policeman picks up his child in his hands and holds him tight, absorbing the lashes of assaults from his knees and elbows, thanking something for his good fortune.

CHAPTER 14

The son watches the night turn to day through the gaps in the green canopy above, forcing him to click off the torch that had been illuminating the manual in his lap. The designs, sketches, instructions, components, parts and pieces all weave together to produce some substance of a plan in his mind, ready for action whatever that may be.

After several hours star-gazing, the dark thoughts and memories had begun to permeate again within. With the embarking of dawn, the son begins consuming the adrenalin and four hours of sleep, starting his journey back into the heart of the city; through the overloaded housing, the grimacing guard at the check point, the white steel and glass tower blocks of the financial quarter, and finally through the bustle of the middle and upper class shoppers in the square, spending their money and downing jars of red wine. In contrast to the day before, the sun begins to break through the clouds to shower the streets with a glorious heat, making the son sweat in his oversized father's jumper.

Walking straight through to avoid another encounter with the policeman, he makes his way off the square again, down the side road, toward the palace where one of the guards in the prison had said the political prisoners would be labouring. Just as he makes the turn between the two restaurants toward the departing street, the son catches sight of the policeman's reflection in the restaurant's large tinted window. For a second, they look at each other nervously, not knowing how to react, with equal perplexity written on their expressions, the policeman standing motionless at the foot of the statue in the centre of the square. He takes a step forward away from the plinth, prompting the son to quiver with panic and walk with haste down the road in the opposite direction, toward the prison and palace.

He passes the jail on his left hand side and blows out a sigh of relief when he sees a different guard from the day before standing at the doorway, albeit with the same aggressive glare and grunt on his acknowledgement.

The son walks toward the presidential palace, toward an equally loud climax of sound as that inside the prison the day before. Cranes oscillate from side to side, carrying large white cubes in the air seemingly light as breeze blocks, with a gathering of people waiting below with arms stretched out, as if worshipping some industrial oracle. The fear of seeing his mother again begins to beat hard on his heart as heavily as his fears of never seeing her at all; that the ex civil servant providing the information to his father in the foreign city was on a quick buck deceiving the desperate and needy, or even worse; that there is some conspiracy to send the dissidents into one area for one quick and silent cull.

The son walks to the wire mesh gate at the site's entrance, where a small white security hutch sits understatedly. He approaches with trepidation, reciting his lines in his mind before rapping on the door. The door eventually swings open to a tall muscular skinhead with no formal attire or weaponry, just paint-dashed jeans and a vest hugging his large rippling torso, partially concealing his myriad of black and red tattoos about his body.

"Yes?" the security officer shouts.

The son, mesmerised by the swirling snake around his left eye socket up to his forehead, looks up without response.

"What do you want?" the security officer repeats impatiently, struggling to fit within the door frame with his wide round shoulders.

"I've come for an inspection," the son says impishly, handing over the pink card, as he begins his government engagement routine, much to the security guard's amusement.

"You want to come in? You know what this place is kid?" the security guard bellows through a chuckle.

The son looks through the wire mesh at a line of inmates shuffling towards a half-dug pit in the ground, each connected by a linked chain around their exposed red ankles. Each of their shaven heads bow down as they motion forward, with arms swaying dejectedly by their sides.

"Yes, I do. I'm ordered to inspect it," the son says, in as formal a tone as he could manage through his gut wrenching nerves.

"Your funeral," the security guard says, squeezing himself through the hutch's door frame.

The son follows as tightly as possible behind the security guard, entering the loud world of industrial engines and yells from foremen and drivers on other side of the mesh gate.

The smell of oil and hot metal instantly hits his nostrils, forcing him to breathe through his mouth to acclimatise, fighting hard to do so without coughing. Making things worse, the security guard lights up a pungent tar-rich cigarette, blowing out the fumes between each syllable.

"Knock yourself out kid. Not that you'll see much. Just boulder on top of boulder, nothing to it. Unless you're looking for something in particular?"

"No, nothing specific," the son replies.

Both of them continue forward, with the security guard shouting commands down some electronic device in his palm, getting cover for the hutch coupled with a series of indecipherable alphanumeric digits.

"So where are you from?" the security guard shouts to him over the noise of a nearby generator.

"The country!" the son barks back, as loudly as his voice box can manage.

"There still people there?"

"Yes. There are still people living that way."

The son catches sight of a group of women in the near distance, shaved and dressed impersonally and asexually.

"What type of people work here?" the son asks in a whimsical tone.

"Only the rebels work here. It's the ultimate humiliation for these types. Imagine! Spend your life trying to break the system and you end up here: building your enemy's palace. Makes you laugh."

"They all look like they're in pain. Everyone is so thin." the son continues.

"They're breaking down their resolve, stripping them of their identity and make them nothing again, like going back to the womb. All principles are broken apart here. They don't get feed or watered until they go back to their cells a day or two later. Most of them end up throwing up or collapsing in front of each other, a total embarrassment, taking away any shred of dignity. They end up fighting each other, stealing, biting and grassing. Any collaboration or camaraderie is torn apart with each passing day. This palace will be built on many broken bones of rebels. Impressive project, no?" the security guard says, with a glimmer of pride.

"Are there a lot of women working here?"

"Yeah, but they're segregated from the men. They get no deferential treatment, if anything they're done even harder. It's not lady-like to be involved with planting bombs and killing people is it?"

The son catches sight of several middle-aged women driving top-heavy pick axes down into the soil, using all their efforts to catch the sharp end into the clay-like earth beneath them. Their pyjama-type clothes stick to their backs with sweat and dirt, with an overbearing uniformed official in shiny leather boots standing on elevated soil in the background, shouting indecipherable expletives at them.

"Hey! Go easy on them!" the security guard shouts at him loudly.

The man swivels round incensed, then brakes instantly on the sight of the guard, with an accompanying wink. The official then turns back to shout twice as vehemently, as if proving his worth in decibels. The son studies the backs of each of the women for signs of his mother, but the impossibility of such a search quickly dawns on him. After so many years out of contact with his own mother, and having not seeing her since such a young age, how was it going to be possible for him to recognise her? From the searching faces in the prison the day before, it would be unfeasible to think that her original features and characteristic expressions would not been distorted, hardened from the stress and torture at the hands of the authorities that kept her here.

The panic begins to eat at the son as he looks at the ubiquitous shape of the backs of the shaven heads, at the hundreds of toiling workers; male and female, young and old, awake and broken. The layer of dirt and sweat in itself is enough to mask the true identity of anyone, let alone the years of sorrow and heartache of hopelessness.

The security guard presses on through the conclaves of working units around the site, functioning as specialised groups doing particular roles, with a respective observer shouting out commands and punishing any and all deviances that harm the efficiency of the task. All of the hundreds of workers begin to merge into one for the son, as he walks around the site with no particular order. The boulders begin to fall atop of each other with perfect precision, climbing up into the sky with a gradual competence, where the immense foundations and number of workers begin to hint at its scale and potential.

"You getting the picture yet, kid?" the security guard asks.

"If you are taking away everything of them then why don't you just kill them? You are reducing them to nothing anyway. Sounds like a pointless exercise to me."

"Then who would build stuff?" the security guard answers defiantly.

"We can."

"You telling me you would work for slop and water?" the security guard asks insolently.

The son looks up at him to take his attention for a second.

"If things are too expensive or too difficult to build, it would look like weakness. There is nothing wrong in admitting something is too complicated. My dad told me that there are some animals that don't know when to stop. They will exhaust themselves in their pursuit until they are spent. True intelligence comes in knowing your limits, right?"

"So you reckon we're animals now?" the security guard laughs from his belly.

The son's façade begins to disintegrate in the face of his anger, at the conditions of the inmates on the site and those still wallowing in the prison. How each of them looks demoralized into something subhuman and destroyed, broken like a toy or car; an absolute destruction of the human spirit and humility.

"I just think this looks like vengeance to me. It doesn't look scientific or sophisticated like you're saying. It may be about stripping their identity and a way of controlling them, but ultimately it is just someone somewhere taking out their pure rage. This palace is beyond humans because it cannot be made without their sacrifice. Ants can make mounds as big as skyscrapers, but they don't because it is beyond the needs of the environment."

Taken aback from the response, the security guard stops in mid-pace, looking down at the son with no expression or words. Seconds pass with nothing but a look, bearing down with an anonymous emotion. Then, without warning, the guard releases a punch at the boy's stomach, sending him flying into the air and then sprawling onto the floor with a cry of agony. Instantaneously, vomit spews from out of his mouth as he wrestles with himself uncontrollably on the floor, trying to endure the pangs of white-hot pain shooting throughout his stomach and chest. Prisoners begin to turn their heads, with subsequent whips and screeches from their observers. The son tries unsuccessfully to haul himself up from the hard floor, a stream of blood trickling from his left nostril and into his gasping mouth. Even the words so aggressively seeking to come out are lost in his failing windpipe, reduced to a faint wheeze lost under the monster engines surrounding him. The security guard picks the boy up from his hair, forcing out a second scream of agony.

"And who are you exactly? I thought this was an *engagement* exercise? All of this is good. Understand it or you get the consequences!" the security guard spits.

The son gets dragged through the site with his heels kicking up the loose rubble in his wake, with an audience of shocked inmates watching on, immobilised by their shackles. He continues to look around despite the burning pain inside, stealing final glances at each one of them in detail, capturing their empathetic faces and gestures. Some bow their shaved heads in grief, while others look on with wide eyed horror, the son taking stock of their engrained hatred for the world they've entered.

Still en route to the exit, gliding past the prisoners face by face, the son catches sight of a particular woman being held back by her observer, with her arms flailing in the air as if positing some psychological breakdown. Her face red with rage and palms open, the son locks his sights on her, grappling with the struggling uniformed man. A second observer strides across confidently and immediately knocks her out cold with a gloved fist, throwing her thin body to the ground and out of the observer's arms. Whilst being dragged past by his collar and hair, the son looks at her face, only ten yards to his side- and suddenly collapses into a state of pure enlightenment, like a switch being flicked from off to on again, with a sudden surge of adrenalin flowing through every limb and his brain flushing with elation.

"Mother!" he tries to shout through an inaudible voice.

The horror of the sight submerges him entirely. He watches

145

his own mother lying bloodied on the floor, with one leg stretched outwards to the connection of her neighbour's shackled ankle and her wide open mouth taking in gasps of breath. Her nose, eyes, jaw line, neck, shoulders, collar bone, chin, each finite feature pieces together to form the hazy memorised image of his young mother, the woman who would bathe and feed him so many years previously, who was now deduced to a heap of unconscious flesh and bones, dominated by strange men in uniforms and batons with gnashing of teeth and drooling spittle.

The security guard drops the son outside of the wire mesh gates and walks round to face him, picking him up by the collar to focus at eye level.

"You want to empathise with terrorists? Next time you come to carry out your *investigation*, perhaps do a little reading upon what they do, all those innocent people they have killed, the women and children they slaughter." The security guard shouts vehemently in the son's face, leaving a trail of spit dribbling down his bottom lip.

"You think there should be flowers and televisions? You want them to read books and learn new languages? They wasted their opportunity for freedom when they burnt down buildings and kidnapped civilians. Now they're good for nothing. The only value they can serve society is what we give them since they're incapable of doing it for themselves. If these places never existed, neither would you, neither would I. They would murder us all to start all over again. They would murder each one of us. You should reconsider this humanitarian crap. If it were me, I'd lock the gates and burn the whole place down and then use their bones for fertiliser."

The son feels his head on the brink of explosion from the swelling noise, and begins to crawl backwards on his elbows, trying to escape further onslaught.

Eventually, the security guard releases his grip and the son is left free to stand up, although not before releasing another puddle of vomit on the grass to his side. He stands up and hobbles on weak knees down the road toward the public square again, past the prison gates to his right and the guard with his institutionalised habit of smoking.

Grimacing in pain and agony, the son walks briskly towards the anonymity of the crowd and weaves between the shoppers to find the straight path, the direction back toward the sheltering canopy of trees, several miles outside of this hell of a city. The only thing guiding each foot in front of the other are the memories of his mother, nurturing him through his childhood with her food, love and smiles, entwined with his father's reassuring hand whenever the situation warranted.

Once resting against the arch of a large oak, he rests his weary head against the hard brittle bark and shuts his eyes, reminiscing heavily to his childhood until his eyes lower and his senses numb into a deep sleep, unaware of the trail of blood still oozing out of his left nostril.

✳✳✳

Out of uniform, the policeman walks into the chattering restaurant with his wife hanging from his arm, towards a reserved table by the window, dimly lit by a dripping candle from a disused wine bottle. Various diners bow their heads in recognition whilst others give a belated wave as they sit down. The celebrity-like status of the policeman draws a proud smile on his wife's face as they settle in their seats and begin selecting from the wine list.

"You choose," the policeman informs his wife, showing a lacklustre interest in the selection.

"You still in a mood?" she enquires of her husband sardonically.

The policeman looks over her shoulder at the calm serenity of the fellow diners, gulping down their lagers and wine carelessly and in free spirit.

"I don't get it," the wife continues. "You have a great job and a borough where nothing happens. Isn't that what you wanted? Isn't that the perfect job?"

"Not here," the policeman says, sliding open the three panelled menu.

The policeman pretends to read the options but secretly retreats back to that obsessive image of the boy in the public square who keeps appearing in and out of the crowds; how earlier on in the day he caught him in pace on the road out of the square with his lanky dishevelled hair and protruding cheekbones from hunger, the dirty ill fitting clothes and strange trail of string hanging from either pocket. Against the backdrop of middle class concerns for consumption and gratification in his district, such poverty shines like a beacon for the policeman, leading him to question the safety which his career choices have landed him.

"You should think about the children more often when you think such things." the wife persists, still looking down at the wine list.

"I do think about them. I want them brought up in a safe environment as much as the next person, that's what got me into the force in the first place. I can actually help bring that about." the policeman responds quietly.

"All those years in the estates, of course you deserve a break!" the wife says.

"Giving directions and putting out illegal cigarettes from kids who have more money than direction?" the policeman says sarcastically.

"You're trying to tell me that you want to go back to those criminals? You want to go back to the projects?"

"You wouldn't understand. When you're in this sort of job, you want to know you're making a difference. I hear from others in the station that things are getting worse in the estates." the policeman whispers from across the table.

"But you just said yourself: there isn't anything going on here! You're doing a good job. So what is the problem?" the wife asks, with a quick glance above the card.

"It won't be long until this sort of irreverence will spill out into the safe zones too; the suburbs; the business quarters. The president has done so much to instil peace and stability amongst our people. He's given our generation a real meaningful path, and focus which for a long time meant that people respected authority. When kids used to see my uniform, they would give me this sort of look. It was as if I embodied the president himself, a kind of representative. Now, they jeer and backchat, all the respect has gone."

"So to win that back, you want to go into the estates and tell them the story of how it all began? I tell you what; they would do a lot more than respect you. You'd be ridiculed. Don't you have any dignity? You tell me that I won't understand. I don't think you get it at all. At the start, everyone walked in the same direction, but now things have got more serious and people are beginning to resent the chastisement, which in turn makes the government more paranoid when people are beginning to talk about other alternatives, and so the grip gets tighter and so on and so forth." his wife says with a straight face.

"So you suggest we let the cycle spiral downwards, since there is no way of stopping it?"

"I don't know how you intend to make things better. This new generation are angry, and you expect to solve it by feeding them with the very thing they despise: control."

"Then why were they so ready at the start? What's changed?" the policeman continues in whisper.

"The government never talked about this sort of governance,

they were talking about lofty ideals and unobtainable utopias. Now all they get is curfew and family planning measures. They are in our houses, our bedrooms, our *thoughts*!" the wife says aggressively.

"Do you think a policeman's wife should be saying this sort of grievance in public? I don't see why you have such objection against the president anyway; do you think our living standards would be as they are without the status quo?"

"I want the best for our family and you know it." the wife snaps back sharply.

"Listen..." she continues, leaning over to gain total focus.

"Things are changing and you can't stop that kind of momentum. You see people scared and paranoid, they're fighting over scraps and they don't trust anyone. But you also see and hear change and that's from the new generation. They don't want to end up like their parents, sitting on either side of the fence – either feeding off the grip on society or being the ones squeezed by it. They just want to be left alone to fulfil their own individual destinies."

The policeman puts his menu down and offers a little wry chuckle to himself.

"You really believe that these dissidents have a valid cause for everything they do? Things are not changing, they are exactly the same. There are two types of people: those who have the means to have what they want legitimately and those that try to get the same thing by illegitimate means; the gifted and the thieves. This has always been the way since civilisation began. There have always been troublemakers trying to purge the riches off of the successful and this is exactly what's going on here, except that in this country some so called *revolutionary* types has come up with notions of rights – that *they* are entitled to these material goods without natural means.

"These people are innately dangerous to society. They fraud their way through life, steal from their mothers, lead perilously hedonistic lifestyles, take drugs and cause disruption. They are anathema to society where no amount of rehabilitation or coaching can fix. They choose the illegitimate means of survival because it is their nature."

"Well, that begs the question what is legitimate doesn't it?"

"Meaning?" the policeman asks with a frowning brow.

"Well, it just sounds like if you're on one side you can get anything you want, but if you're on the other side, you can never get access to it so of course their means are illegitimate. We're towing the line; keeping up appearances; doing what's expected; but that doesn't necessarily mean we're more legitimate than someone who has no option but to take it. It's just because some arbitrary government of the day happens to suggest that some sector of society is entitled and the other half is ineligible."

"That is so cynical," the policeman says, shaking his head.

"So this sudden urge to *correct* a generation is useless, because you're not going to offer them access to jobs and benefits are you? You are just pointing out to them your definition of legitimate behaviour in their own neighbourhood. Don't you see just how divided we are? The only time the government reaches out to those people is through arrest, imprisonment, buying up their food surpluses at unsustainable prices or giving them jobs cleaning the mess from our tables. It's nothing but control and you wonder why there is resentment!"

A young female waitress walks over to the table, unaware of the heated disagreement between the policeman and his wife and folds over a page on her pad.

"Good evening. Are you ready to order?" she asks with a smile.

They both reel off their usual starters, mains and side dishes with an expensive red wine. The husband looks at the waitress writing down the options in elaborate biro loops, and imagines her story, given the heated argument with his wife and her accusations that the new generation are legitimate in their calls for change. He begins asking himself whether the waitress too had come from the countryside to sustain her life with drone-like jobs in the city, and if that engendered some form of resentment towards those people she was serving.

The husband studies the waitress' dyed blonde hair, ruby red lipstick and thick black mascara and contemplates what she really looks like without such a mask; her jet black hair bouncing in the clean autumn breezes of the country, and her fair skin blushing rouge with exertion, rather than pale and provocative in the dirty city she finds herself in. Was the state really *inside* people? Was the state not meant to be guiding the youth to something more idealistic, with an inspirational leader and a bureaucracy to bring about the appropriate changes in society?

The wife returns a smile to the waitress as she leaves with the order, before turning back to her husband.

"Do you think the government could ever be completely at ease with itself? I mean, considering that this *order* you speak of is sustained by force and brutality, how could it ever hope to understand itself as truly benign? The people will never act according to its writ by will because they take away all of the morality involved in their decision making process."

"At some point the people will relate to their material world without reference to any constitution or arbitration by the authorities. It will be pure utopia, without courts and people like me in uniform. That's why we have to give it a chance and work together, not dissolve on the first hint of trouble."

"But how is that ever going to be possible if they don't know what's truly right or wrong? They would only know what's punishable and what's rewarded. Besides, you said that those dissidents are bad because of their nature, so what's the point of even attempting to *condition* them?"

"That is because the future society alone, as an organic and operational unit, will solve itself of rebels and dissidents. When one man decides to run against the grain of natural society that populace would swallow him up to prevent itself becoming weak. A society riddled with rebels is a society destined for self destruction. This government is just a replica of that model albeit artificially, trying to instil those ideas into the people at a practical level to prepare for that society when all laws give way to the natural and principled world."

"So what happens to these dissidents in the mean time?"

"We condition them by stripping away their natural tendencies for hate and destruction, and then teach them the benefits of cohesion and working together."

"Hence the disappearances that all of you keep turning your heads from?"

"Every *disappearance*, as you call them, is followed by investigation helped up by the judicial process."

"The same judicial *process* owned by the government you mean? Can't you see? You call it the bigger picture but it's not the biggest picture. This system wouldn't even be here in the first place was it not for the self-interested multinationals bankrolling the state economy just to keep us out of aligning with our neighbours. You call it principle and design for the future utopia but we are just puppets. They make sure we're fragmented and isolated from the outside world to prevent us organizing and rallying against the super states as a single entity. So many so-called dissidents are lost every day because they don't agree with policy, the same policy which registers their everyday behaviour *illegitimate*. The government defines them illegitimate at birth by their predefined positions in society. If they're rural, intellectuals, relatives of dissidents, acquaintances of dissidents, even cleaners of dissidents, then they're suspects.

"If these people ever organized between themselves with solidarity between our bordering neighbours we would be considered a threat to the global political stability; so it is in the interests of the current world rulers to keep us cut off and fearful. It's absolute paranoia with no end of relief until everyone is in uniform and whistling the same tune. But that is *not* natural society. It's the most artificial, rational, scientific and systematically designed blueprint a human could ever come up with. These ends you keep cooking up can't sustain the means for much longer when the people realise that those billboards and media messages become nothing but a repetitive rhetoric of misguided superiority. Who's the *better* being: the president in his new super palace surrounded by death threats and barb wire; or the solitary man in the field sowing seeds? Nature can't be made artificially, no matter how many policemen are operating in the estates".

The policeman looks at his wife with disdain and shock at the tirade, confused by her sense of anger and frustration before returning back with a hushed insolence.

"The multinational corporations in this country are allowing us a free entry point to international markets for our own goods, raising our wages and living standards. Look at those shops out there, not one of them is domestic. They process our minerals, feed us their food, mend our broken bones, there really isn't anything they don't do for us and you think they are here to keep us contained and in their box? We have grown because of them, not become less significant. Other countries are jealous of our exposure to the world and our risen living standards. We have become three times as efficient as all of our neighbouring countries put together and we import everything from toothbrushes to military helicopters; there is nothing we can't have. Yet you think we have become under their thumb? How wrong you are."

The wife resists a response as the steaming plates are placed each in front of them. She looks at the highly charged electricity of emotion in her husband's eyes, at how the very mention of the government's grand scheme provokes excitement and protectiveness, at the expense of her fears for their family and her own ontological existence.

Throughout the dinner there is small talk between them to fend off the other diners around them, who intermittently look over to see their popular and effective policeman. Whilst in silence, the policeman returns to that image of the child scurrying the streets of his district, questioning his very ideas about the innateness of evil in this new, angry generation.

CHAPTER 15

The phone clicks back into the receiver as the son stares mindlessly at the keypad, studying its contours and corners with a strange concentration, numbed by the sensation of the conversation he had just had. For several seconds he stands motionless, until a rap at the glass door from the other side startles him.

The cool morning air outside forces him to turn his collar up around his neck, and to pull the beanie hat down to his eyebrows. Standing in the bustling public square again, compared to the solitary walk inward from the surrounding woods, always requires a readjustment of his bearings, with a strong sense of being under surveillance by passing shoppers undercover- and more significantly, under suspicion by the policeman circling the pavement several dozen times each day.

The son begins to walk down a specific road leading away from the square, as he had been told to do by the man on the telephone. He settles himself down on a three foot street sign on the corner of a junction, still bubbling up with tension, coupled with a twinge of excitement deep in the recesses of his curdling stomach. The breeze continues to whip his face with a chilling freeze, making it difficult to breathe through his nostrils and just as hard to breathe through his mouth. The houses around him shows signs of destitution and poverty, similar to the zone of overloaded housing on the very edge of the city, where the haunting sounds of family squabbles and children's elation echo through the windows without any signs of life, like ghosts mocking the wanderer. In front of him, a tall housing block rising several hundred feet into the air begins to send out a steady stream of uniformed workers, with different pastel colours and insignias bearing their identities and controllers for the day. Each shares a look of loss and ennui as they form a moving line through the narrow street, towards the public square and the plethora of shops and restaurants.

Still beguiled by the sight of the migration, the son jumps to the sound of a bellow from an opened window of a car.

"Get in!" the man in the driver's side shouts, pointing furiously at the passenger seat.

The son puts himself in the car, taken aback by the rust holes on the floor beside his feet and the riddle of holes in the door to his left, bringing him back to the image of the car in the foreign country which was intended to be their drive to the airport on the day of his father's murder.

"Here you are," the driver says through the side of his mouth whilst staring forwards, handing the son a brown paper bag with the tip of a barrel poking out the end.

The son takes the package in both of his hands, surprised by the weight and awkwardness of the weapon. He looks to the driver, trying to ascertain a judgement of his character.

"Just look ahead." the driver insists.

"And you will wait outside on the hour?" the son asks, trying to take a look from the corner of his eye.

"That depends. Have you got it all?"

The son slides out from his rucksack a wad of notes, almost all of his remaining cash, and places it on the driver's lap.

"I'm not going to be disappointed if I start counting it?" the driver asks under his breath.

"It's all there."

"Where's the device? Are you sure you know how these things work? If you ask me kid, you look a bit young to be dabbling in that sort of thing."

"My uncle put it together. He is an expert." The son lies to put the driver at ease.

"OK then, let's hope so. Next time I'll see you you'll be tailed by a hundred guards, and no doubt for years to come. I don't want you going soft on me, the fee is non refundable. I'm putting my neck on the block more than you are. Understand?"

"Understand." the son says, becoming gradually hit by the brutal realisation of it all.

"The engine will be running facing away the square, so both doors will be ready for you to get in. The car will be at the top of the street so you have to do a little jog, otherwise the heavies will start getting nervous. If they start coming out before you then I'm gone. Understand?"

"Understand."

"OK, get out." the driver says, turning his head towards the son for the first time.

"And I don't need to tell you that you don't know me, right?"

"Right!"

The son retreats back down the street towards the public square, joining the back of the line of workers pushing forward silently as if on some invisible conveyor belt, being deposited into a predefined composite of a machine in the near distance. Some of them blow out smoke above their heads and others tap at electronic devices from the palms of their hands, but all true sense of freedom is shown wanting in their faces and posture, even those with the asymmetric haircuts and subtle tattoos partially hidden by white sleeves seemingly guilty for such individual expression.

At the public square, the son enters a florists, populated by some of the same workers that he had followed down the narrow streets. The scent and peculiarity of the dashing flowers immediately startle the son's senses, and he walks round the shop dazzled. A richly red Dicentra Bleeding Heart bows down on its stem to offers its sweet nectar inches from his nose, whilst potent Blue Roses flirt with his kneecaps from underneath. On the black backdrop of the shop wall, a pale image of Ghost Orchids haunts the room, with star-like patterns floating up and down from the air conditioner in the corner of the room. At the centre of the room sits the centrepiece: a Titan Arum, with a green rod of a pistil shooting up into the air, surrounded by its flurry of dark purple petals. The arbitrary patterns in its folds and contours, and the arrangement of swirling pebbles in its plant pot beneath, begin to train his mind into a excited state of intrigue, as if falling through an ambush cover and down into a hidden world in the undergrowth.

The heady aroma forces memories of his childhood and the kitchen garden that he used to hide within, with its majestic blooming flowers and bursting nutritious fruit dangling above in overhanging trees, peculiar shaped vegetables, buzzing and floating winged insects and the colossal array of land insects that carried out the hidden and unknown fertilisation of the soil. The worms that would tug down the leaves into the wet soggy mud and digesting gulps of earth, leaving enriched castings at the top of the soil for a rebirth of life, along with the white globes of fungi, breaking down matter for the young developing shrubs and trees. For some seconds the son stands transfixed, surrounded by an extension of his own memories; of how the world used to look with his father explaining each and every aspect of the system, showing what did what and why and how. How he would hold petals with delicate large fingers, lift up layers of bark from dead wood to a theatre of swarming insects, each jostling for position, and how butterflies would land on his bare shoulders unhindered.

The son collects a funeral wreath from the back of the shop and walks to the counter, still sharply transfixed by the world around him. The young woman in a pristine white uniform takes the ring of lilies and places it delicately in an assortment of bags to protect the arrangement in transit, then stands looking at the son, awaiting payment with a monotone expression. Her lack of smile or pleasantry is only matched by the son, who passes over his penultimate note with a nervous hand. The worker immediately places the cash in the till, expecting nothing more or less from the transaction, just an everyday standard relationship between some shop assistant and a random consumer.

The son takes flight out of the shop and into the chilling atmosphere of the cool autumn weather in the public square. The people tug their clothes around them tighter to conceal themselves from the whipping breeze, and rush into their destined shops of consumption with haste. As usual, the son captures the attention of the passers-by, attracting suspicious glances and even subtle jeers from his peers.

Aiming for the street that led to the embryonic presidential palace, the son crosses the square promptly, passing under the dark shadow of the overbearing statue in the air and making his way towards the prison he had visited only several days previously. A different guard again standing at the doors makes the son sigh with relief as he passes him as casually as possible, under the heavy thumping of his heart and the racing images circling his desperate mind. As he passes the guard he provides him with an artificial look of a child who had lost a loved one, complete with frowning eyebrows and a conjured tear or two. Counting his footsteps up the street past the door, the son stands twenty feet beyond the guard and bends down to place the wreath of lilacs against the wall, sitting there for several seconds as if in prayer or thought.

Noticing the guard staring at him inquisitively, he takes a second to bow his head further, making the scene seem private and sombre, and drops his shoulders as if in a symbol of hopelessness. Still hunched over the flowers, the son uses restrained, slow, meticulous movements in sliding out the lunchbox from the rucksack he had prepared during the night, packed with a handful of nails, and places it under the ring of flowers, tilted towards the cold red brick of the wall. Pressing down hard on the plastic cover of the box with a responsive click and blinking red light, and then placing leaves over the lunchbox, he stands to his feet again and takes a final bow, before taking an equally sombre stroll back through the street towards the public square again, giving the guard a lasting look of loss and mourning.

The son walks across to the restaurant he had previously visited some days before and takes the same seat in the corner with its optimal view down the junction, in order to watch the standing guard and the funeral wreath propped against the wall.

"Coffee please," the son says to a keen hovering young waiter in black uniform, a worker he had seen come out of the tower blocks that very morning.

The son gulps the air hungrily in hurried fear and trepidation, with his heart continuously beating, making him feel like he is seemingly floating and walking in on himself. *What am I doing here? What if I get caught? What if it ends in her being sacrificed by the government in retribution? What if the driver doesn't come and he is left stranded outside to be cherry picked by the authorities?* The danger of it all begins to settle in his belly like a crown of thorns, as he rifles through the rucksack to retrieve his father's pouch of tobacco and begins rolling with two sweating, trembling hands. The cold breeze hits his wet brow like a blow torch, his constant adjustments in his chair starting to attract attention from others around him.

On the seventh attempt, the son seals off the cigarette and places it in his mouth, trying to fend off the shakes before lighting it, with a steady drag on the tip forcing no cough or struggle but a satisfying pollution of his lungs, to steady his electric nerves and shortened synaptic connections in the brain. A quick glance at his father's watch on his wrist shows a slow-moving minute hand, encouraging the demons in his belly to swoon and swallow more.

The waiter places the cup and saucer on the son's table and leaves promptly, though not before looking down at the ball of anxiety before him, its thin limbs shaking like an addict on withdrawal or a rabbit in the headlights. As the son scans the square around him and the road down to the presidential palace, he spots the tall, moustachioed policeman within the crowd, a dozen shops away on the pavement, talking with hand gestures to a lost pair of tourists. His black authoritative uniform and array of weaponry on his belt sends shockwaves through the son's jittering nervous system from his fingers to his toes. According to his notes and the frequency of the sightings, the policemen was meant to be over on the other side of the square at this specific time of day, several hundred metres away.

The son sits watching, focused on the policeman's every move and direction, whilst dragging on the fast waning cigarette and gulping large mouthfuls of slick dark coffee without milk or sugar. The adrenalin of the moment and the ticking of the watch pulsate like tin barrel drums inside of himself, with an overwhelming panic of worst-case scenarios fading in and out of his brain. Just as soon as the trauma besets him, the moment passes as the policeman leaves the couple and enters a diner close by, a distance long enough to run down the street without capture from the policeman.

The son looks at his watch, with sweat dripping down his back and heart thumping harder and harder inside his elevating ribcage, accentuated by the sucks at the dwindling tip of his haphazard cigarette. Two minutes to go.

The son leaves the table, dropping his last remaining cash note on the table and exiting the seating area of the restaurant. With each foot step towards the prison and the awaiting guard outside, the terror begins to reverberate within him like a conflagration of white hot fear. The son catches sight of the guard looking back at him as he approaches closer and closer. The fear begins to turn into an automatic adjustment of the senses, as if something deep within the recesses of his spirit is conjured up to the surface and floating on adrenalin. Getting closer, the son begins to feel the big right hand of his father's clenched around his own, offering that reassuring glow that only he could give.

Twenty feet away, the son quickens his stride, using his inner momentum to slide his hand up into his jumper and take out the loaded gun acquired from the driver earlier on in the morning, and positions the barrel in line to aim at the face of the guard, making sure to avoid wasting time or a bullet on the body armour within his vest. The guard looks back with a wide eyed expression, trying to claw himself back into the safety of the prison's door and the concrete holding room behind him. But before he can even take a step backwards, the son releases the trigger on the gun and fires a single bullet into the left cheek of the guard, producing an instant jet of blood out of his face and his collapse to the floor, his hand frozen on the holster of his pistol.

The son continues his pace and passes the convulsing body of the guard behind him, writhing and rolling in agony at his feet, to stand within the protection of the archway. Seconds later, the wreath explodes dramatically at the base of red brick wall, a crescendo of red dust and particles of cement dancing backwards in the air onto the street and bouncing off the adjacent building opposite.

The son sprints out from the protection of the archway and towards the remnants of the explosion, with a thick pluming cloud of cascading debris around him and a glitter-like noise as it all falls down against the hard, wet tarmac. Looking round, he notices the public square behind him whirring with the noise of screams and shrieks, some even attempting to run down the street toward him before turning back at the sight of the son's black weapon glinting in the light.

Ignoring the trailing bricks still falling down about him, the son disappears in through the hole made from the bomb. Unlike the public square, the son enters the prison to a still silence, the detainees and guards trying to find their bearings after the shock of the attack. As the dust settles, the son sprints around to the first row of cells on the ground floor where three guards catch sight of him. Struck by the immediacy of it all, and the first howls from the prisoners within their cells, they remain immobile, fumbling at their belts for their pistols. The son aims and shoots at the nearest guard, sending him backwards with a blow to the forehead and swivels to the second, firing at the mouth with a waterfall of teeth catapulting above him. The third reaches his gun and looks ready to pull the trigger, but the zip of the bullet from the son's gun splices through his right hand, two severed fingers falling down onto the ground along with the weapon. A second shot pierces his right eye socket and out through the other side to ricochet against the white concrete wall behind him.

The son looks on at the carnage before him on the concrete floor, fast becoming a pool of blood beneath and spreading along the textured granite. His gun sends off a small trail of smoke up in the air after the shots, with his wrist becoming fused in the holding position and his body trembling from the climax and adrenalin of murder. He walks over to the first guard, with the pulsing jets of blood shooting from his face in an arch onto the floor, and his eyeballs slowly tilting backwards in on himself as if metamorphosing into a zombie in uniform. The second one looks up at the son, still clawing onto the last few seconds of life by seeking some form of mercy from his killer. But the son looks back with a blank expression, showing no sign of empathy or remorse, just a cold, calculated consequence of the circumstances. The gargles of blood drip on either side of the guard's mouth down onto the bleached white shirt, overbearing the insignias on his breast pocket, as he begins to convulse into a spasm before slowly lulling into a similar numb process of death. As each lung collapses, the heart beats its final pulse and his brain no longer transmits signals to his biological system, the law of nature begins to swallow up his rational governance and recedes to nothing but meat and bones in the transit of demise.

The son looks round behind him to ensure no other guards are awaiting him on the upper tiers, then bows down to pick the keys from the belt of the nearest guard. He runs past the cells on either side to a deafening bellow of shouts and screams demanding their release, with some cheering in jubilation as if worshipping a ray of sunshine bursting through a lifetime of darkness and wilderness. The son keeps his focus on the middle of the corridor to the steps leading up to the second tier, where the guard some days previously had explained was set aside for the dissidents. Cups, cutlery and handfuls of food are thrown at him to attract his attention to their plight as he climbs the thirty steps upwards.

He strolls past each cell with a lion-like concentration, craning his neck from side to side to capture the face of every individual. Their faces become a blend of excitement and outright horror at the rapid turn of their fortunes. A boy coming to their rescue with a loaded gun, an intent to murder guards and holding keys to free them from their chastisement. He presses forward between the aisles of cells, scanning every face for the now familiar features of his mother. The shaven heads and ubiquitous uniforms make the hunt more frustrating, every face distorted by gasping mouths, wide eyes, and the constant jostling between cell mates for position at the bars to get the full attention of the boy with the gun striding past.

From memory, the last remaining cells at the end of the cells were empty during his last visit, and therefore those most likely to be sanctioned for the detainees who laboured at the palace. The son begins focusing on the ten chambers at the far side and stands fixed, pivoting on his heels to look in on one cell after another.

Then, just as immediate as the shock of seeing her for the first time was at the palace, the son catches sight of the waling woman, explosive in her intent to grab her own son, her own flesh and blood, as if it were her making the attempt for freedom. Under the thunderous exclamations of her cell mates and throughout the prison itself, he begins to hear his mother for the first time for many years, calling out to him.

"Son! Son! Son!" she bellows out from the pit of her stomach, gravelled by the years of pollution and smog in her weak lungs. A pale limp arm lies outstretched through the bars trying to reach out with an open palm, outspread fingers bearing burns and cuts from the years of hard labour and torture.

The son approaches the cell and fumbles with the keys, trying to find the one with the corresponding cell number inscribed along its column. Hurriedly, and with the pressure of time breathing hot over his shoulder, he eventually finds the key, drives it into the rusty lock and turns it clockwise with a satisfying click before barging at the steel bars with the ball of his right shoulder, opening up the cell with a subsequent clang.

The two inmates sharing the cell immediately take the opportunity and hurl themselves past the son, leaving the exhausted mother slumped on the concrete floor in their wake. Overwhelmed by the sight of her son and the open door, the mother begins to shake within her ill-fitting uniform whilst the son stands above her, gesturing with a guiding hand. As she begins to bawl and hyperventilate, the son takes the initiative and hauls her up onto two tentative legs, starting to motion her out of the cell and down the steps towards the ground floor. Taking note of the jeers and chants from the inmates circled around him behind bars, the son deliberately throws the set of keys into a random chamber, far enough from the inmates to give him enough time to deliver his mother out of the prison without being hindered by the others.

As they both storm through the alley of excited cells on either side and towards the entry point made by the explosives, he catches sight of the two inmates from his mother's cell, disappearing through the hole and out onto the street on the other side. Reassured that the exit route was still available, the son presses forward harder, and begins dragging his mother by her wrist to keep up the momentum. The sound of his mother crying and wailing only adds to the son's sense of urgency, as she begins to resist the charge with a nervous and stumbling pace.

"Quickly!" the son shouts back urgently, not yet used to the commandeering responsibility.

They make it down the corridor of cells and reach the hole amidst missiles of food and bowls. The dust left over from the blast chokes them as they push through the rubble of bricks and out onto the open road. The son looks round to check his mother's condition, as she receptively looks back with an awkward smile, eyes squinting from the contrast of light. The threat of capture or of being shot forces the son to speculate everything, with fleeting glances in all directions. Reassured, he takes his mother's wrist again and runs down the road towards the waiting car, with the driver looking back agitatedly and a pistol aiming at them both for cover. The car begins to reverse up to collect them both with open doors in anticipation.

"Get in!" the son screams to his mother, pushing her in the back of the car and assuming the passenger seat a split second later.

The driver looks back at the woman splayed on the back seat, ankles in the air, and then at the son looking back at him with dilated pupils and gasping for breath.

"Drive!" the son shouts with an adrenalin fuelled rage.

The driver pushes his foot down hard on the accelerator, forcing a high pitched squeal on the tarmac below from the rubber tyres, and drives down the street at top speed. They watch through the back window as the prison behind begins to disappear in the distance, and becomes submerged by figures running down from the square. The driver throws the car down a narrow street on the right before the presidential palace at the end, throwing all three of them to the left inside.

With each winding street they go down the son begins to relax, confident that they had gotten away without detection and without a tail following them. The thrill of the moment is tinged by the total trust placed in the stranger at the wheel whom he had only met that morning, and the real possibility of being set up.

The driver takes the car around a corner at a more comfortable pace, reassured that the danger is now over. For the first time the son turns his head towards his mother, slumped in the back seat in the same position she had entered the car in, face down on the cushion and feet resting against the window.

"Mum!" the son says for the first time.

Just as the syllable leaves his lips, a zipping noise shoots past the son's right ear. Jilted, he looks forward to the driver, at the driver's head tilted back against the chair's headrest. There was no trail of blood upon his face or hint of attack, except for his eyes rolling upwards to the roof of the vehicle. The car veers towards the nearest building on a straight trajectory, cushioned by a brick wall and a nearby row of plastic bollards. They both get hurtled forward and collide with the hard plastic interior. For several seconds there is still silence, except for an alien clicking noise emanating from the engine, and the shifting of position from his mother, wedged behind the front seat, followed by groans of pain.

Stunned, the son checks the driver's throat for a pulse, and in doing so accidentally tilts the head forward on its limp neck. A string of spit and blood spills out of the driver's mouth, along with a trickle of blood from a hole in his forehead, drawing a red thread down the centre of his face and off the tip of the nose. Immediately the son ducks down below the level of the window for fear of further shots, and looks back to his mother; securely nestled between the two seats behind, but conscious.

An eerie silence surrounds the car, and for the first time the son is at a loss for what to do next. Not knowing where the sniper was, or whether their intentions were to kill or capture, passes the situation out of his hands and into some other invisible entity wielding a fatal weapon. For almost a minute, the son concentrates on the dome of his mother's shaven head, pressed down onto the floor to muffle out the noise.

A rage begins to boil up from within, similar to that which galvanised him to turn on the assailant in the foreign country to protect his father. The opportunity of being with his mother again was quickly being lost, within his very hands but being plucked away by the invisible dark forces of authority.

Clasping the gun with both hands, he begins to creak open the passenger door, being careful not to expose himself to the sniper. Except for black and white magpies swirling high in the air, the street remains still and ordered, as he lifts his head above the window frame to take a glimpse down its narrow length. The fearful silence, except for the thumping heart in his trembling rib cage and the muffled movements of his mother in the car, begins to haunt his every delicate move. The street offers no sound or sight of invasion, no cryptic clue as to where the sniper was being concealed. The son sits still on one knee on the concrete pavement and looks down the channel of the street ahead, along the barrel of the pistol. Sweat builds up and drips from his brow, off the fringe of his greasy blonde hair. His index finger trembles in anticipation on the trigger, expecting the assailant to step out for a second shot.

CHAPTER 16

The policeman closes his eyes, holding his posture against the wall to compose himself. The gun, still held aloft in both hands, emits a hot metallic sting in his nostrils. Placing the barrel in his mouth he sucks at the smoke, to prevent it trailing from his hidden position behind the corner. He takes a communication device from his belt and begins tapping with gentle fingers across its keypad, informing his colleagues of his location and situation. Confident of the situation, given the condition of the car and the accuracy of the shot to the driver, he begins to inch nearer to the edge of the building's corner. Using the hazy reflection of a nearby window the policeman watches the car with its passenger door open. Only fifty feet away, the sound of the vehicle's engine clicking is the only thing that can be heard, nothing else in motion except for the shadow of whirling birds above the roof tops. He shifts on his heels to get closer to the corner's edge, with the barrel of his pistol inching forward.

The policeman steps out from the safety of the building's edge and approaches the car with tentative steps, gun in both hands and fixed towards the vehicle's windscreen. Then, after several steps forward, a crown of blonde hair rises up behind the passenger window.

"There is a gun on you, do not move or I'll shoot. Stay where you are and raise your arms into the air!" the policeman barks aggressively at the stranger.

The top of the stranger's head begins to rise up behind the

glass. Both of his hands follow suit; one wielding a glinting pistol and the other an open palm of surrender.

"Drop the gun. Now!" the policeman shouts.

It is not long before the policeman identifies the stranger as the boy who had collided with him in the public square, who had been frequenting the area with a strange intensity for the past three days. The young almond face with large hollow eyes, constantly in bewilderment yet also fatigued by struggle, looks back at him with a cold and fearless expression, a far cry to how he was in the public square. Silence cascades between them as they peer deep into each other's eyes to gauge intention. Holding the gun at eye level, ready to send a bullet through the boy's forehead, the policeman's right hand begins to subtly tremble uncharacteristically. The face that had so forcefully engulfed him for so many days with intrigue; making him redress his very notions of the new dissident generation, plaguing society with violence and revolution.

"I'm not alone," the boy informs the policeman, pointing to the back of the car.

"Who else is in there?" the policeman asks.

"My mother."

"Is she carrying a weapon too?" the policeman asks, trying to steal a glance through to the back seat of the vehicle without giving an opportunity to the boy.

"No."

"I said, put the gun down. What is all this about?" the policeman asks, dropping his guard very slightly to give the impression of empathy.

The boy looks back blankly, still holding the gun aloft in the air.

"Is this why you've been here for so often these days?" the policeman continues. "Planning?"

Again, the boy keeps his steely gaze not dropping resolve or position. The policeman takes the opportunity to size up and assess the situation; on whether there were other terrorists in the car, if the boy was carrying strong enough explosives to decimate the pair of them or whether this was just a minor attack within a grander revolutionary movement sweeping through the city in which case to shoot and flee would be the best option. Or was this nothing more than a son redressing a miscarriage of justice.

"You dropped something behind in the square when you bumped into me, remember? You remember me, right?" the policeman says, as he takes out the Hessian sack of seeds from his pocket, something that had remained there ever since he picked it up from the wet pavement and watched the son run off towards the crowds.

The policeman throws the sack in front of the passenger door, spilling out a dozen dancing seeds on the tarmac in momentum. The son looks down at them, as if insulted by the gesture.

"I'm taking my mum home." The boy finally relents, breaking

his silence.

"But she is a prisoner. They are in jail for the safety of others. They will be freed when they no longer pose a threat. You understand that, right? We do not give clemency to anyone whoever they are. We cannot give preferential treatment to anyone. I am sure whatever she has done she is learning from it, and will be out through in no time through the legal due process," the policeman continues, with a contrived plea for understanding.

"She didn't do anything. She is my mother."

"I know. I understand, but I just want to remind you that whatever the state does, it is for the good of everyone, including your mother. I know you can't see that now but she is learning from her incarceration. It is good for her. Imagine if we didn't have such a process? There would be people murdering each other all over the place. You wouldn't want that would you? Who knows if we'd be standing here right now if it wasn't for such a public service? There is a grave threat posed by a certain types of people in this society that are trying to push you down the wrong road. They want to equip you with the will and the means to kill and harm other people in the community."

"But this government killed my father and he wasn't part of this *type* of person. He didn't want to be part of your war. So tell me, who protects us from the *protectors?*"

"We only bring down terrorists, you should know that from the newspapers." the policeman reasons sharply.

179

"Really? You're the one pointing the gun at a child." the boy retorts, beginning to become infuriated by the distraction of debate, preventing their escape out of the city and into the safety of the countryside.

The son turns round to look at the back seat of the car and sees his mother lying in a foetal position, knees tucked in with wiry forearms, trembling in fear.

"Listen. I know why you would feel this anger at us but you have to imagine the alternative. Before we came along there were people steeped in poverty, there were people in the country that died from plagues and drought. But now we protect these people from these dangers with science and rational thought. We irrigate the soil so farmers can continue producing their harvest for the good of the people, we fend off plagues using affordable chemicals; it is a society where no one is poor because we are all operating as a collective, like a single person. Doesn't that make you feel proud about where you come from? How your government has designed an organism in which every atom is included and all external threats are destroyed. And you are part of it, as is everyone you see in the street. We are one."

The boy continues to look back at him with a passive expression as the policeman steps closer.

"But of course, there are sacrifices. You have to understand that some human beings have something inside them which, when free to express it, can endanger the very world we are enjoying today. Some people are naturally inclined to murder, others are hard wired to steal, even some to rape children! So it is our responsibility as a government to ensure that we make these people *free* from these inherent desires by altering their urges with thoughtful processes. When these don't work, then obviously we have to contain them as best we can, but through a diligent legal process to ensure that their rights are upheld. So I'm sure your mother has exhausted all such steps and admits guilt to her misdemeanour, whatever that may be."

"What if you shot me now? What justice would there be? You would get honoured for bravery and I would end up as yet another example of a terrorist *fixed* by the system. The people that murdered my father are walking free whether they get caught or not." the boy says defiantly.

"To construct this society requires some form of legal immunity, otherwise it could lead to the hierarchy that protects us toppling over on itself. Imagine if the president was suddenly struck down by some malicious campaign to undermine him, how would the country survive?"

"But I'm not talking about fraud or untruths. I'm talking about peoples' lives. I'm talking about my own parents. I'm talking about me." the boy says, beginning to lower his hands.

"But you have nothing to worry about if you have done nothing wrong, right? You can be part of the people, that works hard and benefits from the fruits of society," the policeman says, keeping his hands on the gun.

"But you just said that there are certain evil people who are uncontrollable that only the state can remedy. So what choice do I have? I'm either evil or I'm a fully fledged citizen, with no space in between."

"As a policeman it is important to be able to judge situations before they happen and a big part of that process is deciphering the people involved and their intentions. Their shifting eyes, the clothes that they wear, how they respond to certain circumstances within their surrounding environment, their behavioural patterns, their responses to certain other types of people especially those in authority, even how they write or walk within the cracks in the pavement, everything can be used to reduce a human being into a sizeable formula."

"And?" the boy asks blankly.

"From the first time I saw you in the square several days ago I could spot a mile off that you had been exposed tragedy from your neurotic behaviour; how you would dart from side to side on the pavement with the paranoia of being caught by something or someone, playing with bits of string in your pockets for some endemic comfort and how a police uniform causes instant shock. This isn't the behaviour of a terrorist." the policeman informs the boy abruptly.

"And what about your own evaluation? The need to have shining boots, an arsenal of weapons around your belt, a bullet proof vest and a series of digits for a name?" the boy asks.

"It is impossible to just be a man of authority. When I put my uniform on I don't have an identity. My personal taste in music, my favourite wine, my preferred choice of colours, all are forgotten in the name of appropriating the government and its duty. That is why I am here helping you because it is my role to serve the people and make society the best it can be. You have to understand this."

"And what does it say about someone who wants to work for a government that disappear people? Doesn't that say more about you?"

"It is an honour to serve your country. It's providing something back to the very thing that made us. Isn't that the ultimate dream for any man?"

"After what the state has done to these people do you honestly think they would want to have anything to do with it, let alone serve it?"

"The president is as much everyone's as he is mine. From the lonely post box to the biggest anti tank missile, everything is designed and implemented in the pursuit of making society the best for everyone equally."

"But that's crazy. We are not all the same. You said yourself that some people are inherently evil and some are good. How can we all be the same if we're at the same time different?"

"Exactly! It is something we are trying to *create*. With a little bit of thought these differences can be ironed out to make our social world equally bountiful for each individual and the whole society more easily governable. For centuries policy has revolved around serving the interests of divergent pockets of minorities rather than a cohesive whole. So much alienation and mistrust between these groups. Why do you think there is so much war and violence? Imagine a world with one identity and one destiny. All conflict subsumed by peace!"

"Then why are so many people in this country fighting with each other? For food and shelter and any scrap of territory. No one trusts anyone." the boy says coldly.

Whilst listening, the policeman slides his hand covertly into his pocket and begins tapping the message '*Controlled*' on the communication device, whilst retaining an eagle-like focus on the boy down the barrel of the pistol. Despite the deep engagement with the nervous boy, the sense of danger still reverberates through his chest and stomach.

"Listen to me now. You know the right thing to do. If you give your mother over now you can go back to your home and she will be able to return to her cell without any punishment or consequence. The alternative is for you to carry on with a gun in your hand threatening a police officer and you will end up in the same place as your mother. How would that ever help her?"

"There is a third option. You have already destroyed our lives and thousands of other families. You think the right thing to do is to just walk away? No, you leave us alone. You threaten us with your bloody hand of your law whilst we burn ourselves out producing and servicing the wealthy. This is no society it is a torture garden for your own pleasure. You talk about right and wrong and how some of us are forever evil because of where we come from. But you are forgetting something; we are all exposed to the most horrific violence, sin and corruption from your government that we have become rendered as animals. The state has made me. You have made me. You said yourself that you lose all sense of identity when you put on that uniform, that you become the president himself, a personification of his very ideals and designs.

"We were once free to make our mistakes and learn from our wrongdoings, but now we are governed by some thug police force that takes away our ability to be free. All we know now is evil and what actions avoid further brutality at the whim of a president. No good exists anymore. When you in your uniforms murder my father, imprison my mother, hound us in foreign cities with the aid of your fund raisers in the multinationals and now point a gun at me, what do you expect to happen? The duty and responsibility given to you by us has been bent out of shape and made into something that suits the interests of your president. You only infer kindness in my face because that was a virtue given to me by my father except that you have now stolen that from me and replaced with blood, poison and violence. Don't you ever wake up in the night and think of your role in this system? What you're doing? What harm you do to our fellow people?"

The policeman lowers his gun slightly, dumbfounded by the articulate words coming from the boy, starting to turn slightly rouge with the passion of his vitriolic tone.

"To build a strong society requires a strong cohesive identity which is created and maintained by the president and the president only. In the end, you will be part of something new and powerful, famous around the world for a model of governance where each individual is as significant as the next. This is why I do what I do. I'm helping to create something special where my own children can enjoy a sophisticated high education, a fulfilled and well respected career and a clean and safe neighbourhood for their own children. This is why you should hand your mother over now, to make sure this road is abided to. We are not evil. Look at us now. Why am I not shooting you now?"

"But you are killing people because they have a different opinion. Paranoid to the point that you think these alternatives lead to a domino effect that will topple over your house of cards. You even murder people who don't have an opinion at all and those who choose to stay out of the system completely because you don't understand them. My father wanted no part of this conflict between all of these self interested parties, and wanted to remain stuck where he was, rearing his children and toiling the soil as his father had done before him."

"If you hand over your mother you can go free and live the same way as your father did. Providing you pose no threat to our project, there is no reason for you to be in any danger from the state."

"But how do you expect me to believe that? So many people

are murdered every day for the most menial of reasons that it just becomes an orgy of paranoia and suspicion; of people that look or sound or walk *like* a dissident. Why don't you just shoot me? No one would know it is you, the street is empty and you can report it as self defence."

The policeman begins to panic on his feet, watching the boy become energetic in his oratory. The thought of killing a child for voicing his resistance begins to curdle in his belly, making him feel queasy and sick. The policeman starts to calculate the chances of the boy handing over the mother, weighing them against the risks of him firing his pistol.

"Where were you going?" the policeman asks of the boy.

"Away from here, that is all you need to know."

"With an intention to come back with more explosives?"

"You think I'm a terrorist? You think I have an ideology running through me? I want my mum back. Don't you get it? You took her away from me, like my father, now I'm piecing it back together again."

"It is much easier to destroy a dream than it is to build one. Do you know this? A seed of doubt or a slight chink in its hypothesis can bring it all crushing down until the architects are exposed for vengeance. But with perseverance and commitment a dream can come true and it can be magical. Now you understand why I cannot let you go?"

"Even at the expense of so many people and their livelihoods, their identities? I would like to see you suffering on the other side; your wife and children drowning under the pressure of your own creation. Where the state will come knocking at your door expecting servitude or death; your produce under the thumb of state management; your lifestyle scrutinised by councils and educators; the constant sacrifice of your very being in order to become suited and booted for the *cause*. Would you be proud of your son if he followed the same path as you? Or a secret police informant; picking off suspects because of the current blacklist of the day? You talk about my human nature, what about yours? You've become so immersed in the system that the system has become your flesh and blood. Do you know what is immoral anymore or just what is legal? Standing here right now, with a loaded weapon on my head; is this the dream? A true means to an end? Just question yourself and you will realise that I shouldn't offer us up to you, but you should let us free."

The policeman shivers from the cold sweat trickling down the inverted groove along his spine. Along with the urgency of the situation and the risk of someone coming round the corner, authority or citizen, the policeman begins to round off his decision-making process. A city on red alert looking for a terrorist and his hostage would either leave the boy dead or with a prison sentence stretched beyond his natural life. The policeman soon realises that he is the boy's only ticket out by turning a blind eye, but to do so would be putting his wife and children in danger from state reprisal. For the first time the question of righteousness seeps in before the law as he begins processing the arguments from the young boy before him. Perhaps he was right; perhaps the problem lies within the hands of the government itself. The more the government tries to reverse the problem, the more it widens in scope.

The policeman looks down along his arms to the gun clasped in two trembling hands and at the boy standing in its crosshairs; his dishevelled lanky blonde hair and two large nervous eyes staring back at him. As if walking in on himself, he begins to feel a dizzying sensation of guilt at the pit of his stomach. Years of training in the forces to kill and maim any potential threat to the project begin to dissolve at the feet of a boy whose demeanour and intentions are unknown. Images of his sons flicker in and out of focus in a quickening state of delirium, as his heart races like a drum roll and his arms waver in the air. A cold sweat drizzles down his back and chest from the stifling collar of his uniform as he tries to regain composure and refrain from falling. The son looks back, confused.

"You bought this war to me. I'm not here to bring down your buildings, your banks or your palaces. I'm only here to bring my mother back and now I have got her. You stole her from us in your campaigns and then you murder my father. I may have done something illegal in your eyes but I have not done something wrong. You were right when you said that there are some things in all of us which we cannot suppress. Something deep within ourselves that binds us together despite any sort of trial or tribulation. This is exactly what I am doing now; you can see that force right in front of you now and it makes you nervous. I'm standing in your firing range knowing I could take that bullet for her. That is something your state and your administration cannot handle, because it's a power you cannot control or harness. That's why you took my mother away; to deconstruct her by removing the thing that makes her what she is: a mother, a husband, a friend, a sister, a gardener."

The policeman feels a buzz from the electronic device in his pocket, ringing hard for attention. Defeated and exhausted, the policeman lowers the gun a few degrees and then searches for the device from his pocket before speaking in a deep monotone.

"Target is heading to the square, repeat, target heading to the square. Reposition all officers immediately," the policeman says through the crackling static.

The boy looks at him, unsure of the policeman's intentions as he watches him put the device back in his pocket, but with one hand still on the pistol's handle.

"I will shoot unless you leave here as quickly as possible. You keep walking on down that road you were heading to and continue until out of this city. I'm never going to see your face again in this district and you have never seen me."

The boy takes no second chances and darts back inside the car. His mother, still enclosed between the two seats, looks up blurry eyed as if waking from a deep sleep. All the time checking the policeman's position, the boy begins to guide his mother out with his right hand as she struggles with her limbs and the confined space.

"Quickly, we have to go!" the boy demands quickly, reaching in to grab his mother's wrist.

The mother responds sheepishly and clambers out of the car haphazardly with weak legs. On standing upright from out of the car and catching sight of the uniformed officer across the street she freezes in motion.

"It's OK, he's not going to shoot," the son says calmly.

Both of them walk cautiously away from the vehicle under the gaze of the policeman, who alternates his aim between the pair of them. The long walk for them to the junction and out of the road takes an age, with each stride a step closer to freedom and a trample over the policeman's concept of truth and integrity.

He watches them disappear around the corner with the gun still held aloft in limp wrists, contemplating what had just happened and the consequences of letting them go. Hazy images of his three sons appear again in his thought process, leaving a sense of gratitude and longing to be close. Only with the memory of their smiles and laughter does his racing heart simmer and settle, as he lets the gun drop to his side.

Another call comes through the device, startling his frame into consciousness. The policeman quickly hushes the vibration and puts it to his ear. The sight of the empty street ahead with the silent swirling birds above makes him want to retch, but he still tries to maintain composure for the incoming call. Words spill out from the ear piece without meaning amongst high pitch crackles and a voice desperate for attention. A minute passes as the noise increases in tone and volume, with no response from the policeman, who stands immobile, still transfixed at the son and mother's exit from the throat of the empty street.

The policeman drops the phone to the floor, shutting off the noise with a definite crack against its plastic casing, and then walks towards the car in a trance. He stops short and picks up the Hessian sack which had been thrown during the negotiation, raising it against the sunlight above. The natural light catches the infinite fibres coating the bag and the few seeds emanating from its tears, as some fall to the ground to dance on the black tarmac. The rough texture against his smooth hands makes the grip more satisfying, warranting a tighter squeeze, and in turn allowing further seeds to fall chaotically to the floor.

Beguiled, the policeman watches them in meditation, with a pattern of shadows spiralling around the protected embryos from the hungry birds above. Such understated objects of life as a bunch of seeds capture his spirit as much as the child had done for several days, with his intense eyes and awkward gestures. The dark almond shaped acorn seeds, the dainty butterfly wings of the maple seed and snail like cypress seeds all intermingle inside the palms of his hands, with hypnotizing autumn colours and spellbinding shapes.

The policeman places the sack of seeds back inside his pocket and walks past the car towards the adjoining street, leading up to the square from which the vehicle had come. The long walk back passes by in a haze, with concerned citizens double-taking at his dishevelled face and nervous disposition. As the policeman reaches the last road toward the square, his stupor is unsettled with the sight of commotion and bright blue lights whirling around the prison's entrance. Red bricks litter the road in a dozen-metre radius from the wall, and a concentration of officers crowd the area within the boundaries of yellow flapping tape. As he approaches, he watches two head-shaven inmates being painfully delivered to the ground with their hands bound behind their backs. Intermittent officers look up and acknowledge the policeman with a sombre nod as they interrogate the two men. At the other end of the street lies the public square, and a crowd of civilians looking on with shock over the shoulders of security officers with batons and gas.

Several officers and investigators in suits approach the policeman with severe expressions, hurried in their gestures.

"Where have you been?"

"I caught up with him by short cut. Shot him in the head. His body's still in the car but I don't think you'll get much out of him." The policeman says defiantly.

"You killed the terrorist?" the assumed chief of officers asks.

"What did you expect me to do?"

"Was there anyone else?"

"He was the only one."

"You'll be retiring on a nice little pension for this, that's for sure."

The policeman reassuringly massages the Hessian sack of seeds in his pocket as he leaves the circle surrounding him and towards the hole in the wall where the son had captured his mother. For the first time the noise and smell of chaos begins to unnerve his senses, as investigators documents the rubble with strobe lights and flash cameras. The smell of chemicals in the air stings his nostrils and chokes the back of his throat, galvanising a desperate need to escape and gasp for clean fresh air.

CHAPTER 17

The son navigates through the winding streets towards the general direction of the outbound road of the city, through the financial quarter and housing projects on the outskirts. Walking alongside his mother, he intermittently turns to steal a glance at her, shaven head bowed to the floor, without a word except for an occasional sigh. Her silence and vague eyes disturb the son, intermingled with the excitement of her presence after years of longing. For now the loss of his father's hand is confused by the proximity of his mother, and her shell-like existence.

"We have to keep tight," the son says to his mother in a gentle pitch.

The son watches her thin arms and bulbous elbows swing loosely with each of her strides, clanging against her over-defined hips as she struggles to keep pace. He watches her head focused on the pavement, looking heavy in relation to the thin shoulders and neck supporting its weight. Noticing the cuts and bruises lining her forearms, and a deep indentation on her forehead, makes the son feel ill and forces the question about her plight in prison; the torture of being incarcerated, enduring hard labour, the loss of her family and the humiliation of deprivation. Whether consumed by anger or from a glowing gratitude, the son struggles to understand her temperament. The words struggle to take form as he attempts conversation.

In the silence, he retreats back to the comfort of his

memories; how he spent time with his mother in happier times. Helping her press lemons for the cool lemonade that his father would come in and gulp in glassfuls; grinding heather to infuse the hot melting paraffin wax that they would then both sell in the bustling market a half day away in the nearby town. Even the simple idea of her reading stories from dusty books and dirty fingers from the toiling in the kitchen garden is enough to force a subtle smile on most days. However, the son cannot hide his disappointment in what his mother has become, inverted and vacant, considering the journey and sacrifice in getting her back.

The silence continues through the straight road and the tall skyscrapers of the financial quarter, glimmering with glass and shimmering steel. Only to the eerie backdrop of the housing projects on the city's outskirts, and its ghostly whispers from behind closed doors, does his mother react. As she cranes her neck upwards to look at the decrepit houses, the son is able to catch sight of the true extent of her downfall in the bruises that colour her face.

As was now standard, the son brandishes the pink card to the gateway security officer and delivers the usual explanation about the government inspection initiative which provides freedom of movement in and out of the city. All the time the mother remains focused on the ground, avoiding eye contact with the stranger as if ashamed of her condition. It takes a gentle tap on the shoulder and a guiding hand to show her the path through the checkpoint and out of the city.

The guard watches quizzically as the son panders to his

mother's resistance, and tries to coax her toward the hill several hundred yards ahead, the dividing line between the city and the country. The steep ascent proves nearly impossible for her delicate frame and wasted muscles, as she winces audibly with pain. Even with an arm around her shoulders bearing her weight, the effort only demonstrates the damage done inside.

An hour passes in the evening's dawn, until they both achieve the final descent to the bottom of the hill and the first columns of wide oak trees. The son looks round at his mother who collapses nonchalantly against a cushion of leaves and breathes heavy gasps into the cool autumn air.

"We will rest here. This is a safe place and it will be dark in a few hours, OK?" the son assures his mother.

The mother looks back despondently through narrow eyes, looking as if trying to understand her fate by the expressions on his face. The son takes out his father's large jumper from the bag and places it around her shoulders and waist, to fend off the breeze tracing through the filter of trees behind them. It is not long until the silence and loss of light brings about an atmosphere conducive to sleep, and her eyes begin to droop in response. The son sits with the arch of his back against the bark of a tree and salvages the remaining light of dusk to analyze his mother and her endless catalogue of cuts and grazes.

The temptation to sit nestled under her arm, or to lie next to her broken body for warmth and comfort, begins to sit uncomfortably alongside a yearning to intimate with her the years of searching and struggle that he and his father endured to come find and free her. That she had not asked about the fate of her husband or about where her son had been living, given the government crackdown on dissidents and associates, begins to frustrate him to the core. Had she forgotten the capacity to empathise and love in that lightless dungeon? Had love been beaten out of her? Similar to the previous nights in these woods, the son sits up alert as night falls, with a complementary warm gentle breeze flowing through rustling treetops above, sending down spiralling leaves around their bodies.

The moonlight casts a mysterious shadow on his mother, with the sphere of her shaven head and hollowed tired eye sockets. The reminiscing on his childhood continues to flow in and out of his consciousness; of his mother and father wrapping him up in an orb of warmth and safety, and then just as quickly, the stabbing pain of watching it all smashed to pieces by men in black uniforms and truncheons. Owls in the near distance begin to hoot, along with a delicate hissing of the crickets singing in the bog outside of the woods. The son begins to feel himself fall into the hands of a deep sleep decorated with fantasy and memory, love and violence.

The initial lull and warm dreams soon turn into aggressive fits of fictitious torture and death as the son lashes out around him. A direct collision between his fist and the nearest tree stump transports him back sharply into a hot and sweaty consciousness, with a morning light burning his eyes. A string of spit covers his face where his head had been turning violently, with a fresh wound opening up on the knuckles of his right hand, informing the son that he had been hitting out without knowing whilst still asleep on the leaf laden floor.

Frightened by his own unknown potential, he immediately looks over to where his mother had been resting the night before to affirm her safety. An effervescent panic builds up from his stomach as he looks at his father's jumper, tossed dejectedly against a branch of a nearby birch, with the area where she had been sleeping now empty. The son gets to his feet and begins kicking furiously at the fresh tree leaves where she had slept, searching for some hidden clue. The thought of the authorities coming in the middle of the night to recapture their prisoner fuels his desperation, as he manically dusts the soil of leaves and twigs. He throws himself down in exhaustion and tries to wail into the air, but the hard wind swallows the volume furtively. A stinging pain consumes him as he picks up particles of earth before grinding it hard against his face, smearing the soil along the contours of his cheeks and forehead and then into his mouth, as if eating the world that taunts him.

With his head pounding, the son collapses to the ground in a heap and allows his eyes to meander solemnly around the woods at a worm's eye view. The tall swaying trees bash their thick branches against each other high above, and entangle their branches to conceal the sky. A red fox, a hundred yards in the distance in a clearing, can be seen sinking its teeth into a carcass of a weaker species with its hind legs still kicking out in futile defence, its lower intestines spilling out in all directions around the predator's blood stained fangs.

The son claws himself across the floor with searching hands in amongst the whirlpool of spinning leaves, grabbing his bag for the gun. Driving his hand down to the bottom, he rifles through the objects for the cool sensation of the pistol handle but instead reaches only malleable clothing and food. He begins throwing manuals, chemical bottles and bread rolls around him, then tips the bag upside down to litter the floor with the smaller knives and electronic wiring from the bottom. The disappearance of the weapon jilts the son even more, forcing him to hurl the empty bag to the floor.

The branches continue to crack and groan under the strain of the prevailing wind as he clambers to his feet and stumbles to the perimeter of the woods. Looking upwards, the son watches the slow moving grey clouds swooning towards the lone sun in the centre of the sky, casting a shadow across the ground and his upturned face. Spanning the countryside, the son suddenly catches sight of a thin figure, struggling with the ascent of the hill a hundred feet above. The awkwardness of the movements quickly informs him that it is his mother, trying to surmount the hill as quickly as possible.

The son stands stoically against the beating wind, his shirt being pulled against his body and his lanky hair whipping across his brow; a still statue of a boy resiliently taking on the world, his spirit progressively numbing. Any notion of identity or character quickly disappears over the hill, destined for the big, dirty city beyond with a gun, and a resolve and thirst for vengeance deeper than kinship. As he watches her thin skeletal frame navigating the terrain with fumbled footsteps, the son merely captures every second for memory's sake, knowing it would be the last he would ever see of his mother. Inside, he begins to picture the carnage she was about to place on her captors, and whatever cause she was to let grow within her, sprouting outward in her tenacity and intent to wreak revenge.

The mother gradually disappears from view, leaving her son standing under the opening clouds of rain and thunder. Several hours pass with lightning pounding his senses, drenching his clothes in a downpour of fast and fat rain. It is only when the clouds part, and the sun re-emerges, that he turns from the hill and faces the woods again. The walk through the trees and out onto the open plains of the countryside takes a day, without rest or water. Throughout the journey, a falcon rides the thermals high above his head, tracing his route tirelessly until the boy reaches the safety of the house that he was conceived and reared in.

***

The policeman struggles to carry himself over the uneven landscape of the hill whilst his three sons dart past him and through his legs to take the lead. The sunshine beaming on their faces makes the effort twice as vehement. Panting and wheezing, the peak of the hill seems increasingly distant, not helped by two of his children jumping relentlessly at his back and tugging at his ankles.

The descent sends a thrill of excitement in the children as they throw themselves down in tumbles, running at speeds beyond the momentum of their legs, sending them tripping over fast and furiously down the hill, making light work of the walk. The laughter and shrills of delight from his three sons make the policeman glow and grin, engendering in him his own adolescent free spirit as he charges down rapidly to a rapture of yelps from the foot of the hill and the outskirts of the woods before him.

After several hours of rushing in and out of the luminous green canopy of new leaves above and the crunch of the golden fallen ones under foot, all four of them return back to the clearing outside of the woods.

"Watch carefully," the policeman says, as all four huddle round.

He brings out a trowel from his back pocket and delivers a sudden stab at the ground, making the blade sink to half its length into the soil before wriggling it to make a precise hole and depositing the surplus to one side. Doing this three times, he captures the imagination of the boys as they watch the strange process with intrigue. Taking from his pocket the Hessian sack that he picked up from the boy in the square several months ago, he starts to sprinkle seeds in the palm of his left hand and offers it to his sons, to pick one each with a thumb and forefinger.

"Drop them to the bottom of the hole and then slide the soil back over it," the policeman informs them, watching their eyes darting between the holes and each other.

"What will it do?" one of them asks.

"It will make one of them," the policeman replies, pointing to the bountiful woods behind them.

Each of them begins dropping their seeds into their respective holes and hungrily covers it with soil using grubby hands.

"Then, using the palm of your hand, pat the soil down to make sure it's tight and compact. Like this."

They each in turn look up at their father and try to grin through the bright light of the sunshine above. The policeman beams back and opens his palm of seeds again for the taking.

"Now, we do the same for the rest."

www.ingramcontent.com/pod-product-compliance
Lightning Source LLC
Chambersburg PA
CBHW030319180626
46810CB00003B/1151